HOLMES OF THE MOVIES

HOLMES OF THE MOVIES

The Screen Career of Sherlock Holmes

DAVID STUART DAVIES

Foreword by Peter Cushing

NEW ENGLISH LIBRARY
TIMES MIRROR

This book is dedicated to my mother who took me to see
my first Holmes movie
and
to my wife, Christine, who is 'the woman' in my life.

First published in Great Britain by New English Library,
Barnard's Inn, Holborn, London EC1N 2JR in 1976

Typesetting by South Bucks Typesetters Ltd
Printed by Thomson Litho, East Kilbride
Bound by Hunter & Foulis, Edinburgh

450 03358 9

Contents

Foreword

With the current plethora of books appertaining to films, it was inevitable that one should be dedicated to the most famous detective in fiction. Fortunately, this task has been undertaken by a writer who not only possesses profound knowledge of his subject but also has deep affection and regard for it.

His brief biographies concerning some actors who have interpreted Sherlock Holmes, combined with resumés of certain scripts, make fascinating reading, and a unique reference book for all those who find pleasure in this 'unwanted child' of Conan Doyle's creative genius.

The author explores the many innovations made by various producers who have attempted to 'ring the changes' over the years in order to attract fresh audiences to the cinema. But nostalgia is a strange and potent force, filling even those too young to remember certain eras with a longing for times gone by, and the original sixty stories still hold the greatest power at the box office and in our hearts.

With a firm yet gentle hand, Mr Davies guides his readers to this conclusion, leaving them with the comforting certainty that Holmes and Watson will never die, and, unlike the old soldiers in the song, they will not even fade away.

Peter Cushing,
Whitstable, Kent.

Chapter 1

Sherlock Holmes: An Introduction

WHENEVER cartoonists or comedy scriptwriters wish to lampoon the art of crime detection they grace their characters with a deerstalker and a magnifying glass. They are in fact participating in the proliferation of the Sherlock Holmes legend, as we do also whenever we sarcastically prefix an answer to a query with the words, 'Elementary, my dear Watson'.

The potency of the Holmes myth is verified by the commissionaire of the office block which now occupies the site of 221 Baker Street, where Holmes supposedly shared rooms with Dr Watson. Each year he receives various enquiries concerning the master detective, ranging from, 'Was he a real detective?' to 'Do his rooms still exist?' The Abbey National Building Society which covers 219 to 233 Baker Street receives every week a bundle of letters addressed to Sherlock Holmes. They are courteously answered: 'You will appreciate that Mr Holmes had to vacate his rooms and unfortunately we do not know his present whereabouts.'

Despite the fact that even if Holmes were alive today he would be well over a hundred, the letter writers are not deterred; it may well be as one London teenager wrote, 'Perhaps you should wonder why a sensible and quite sane school girl should write to you? It is because you are immortal.'

And so a man who never lived, lives on. Why is Sherlock Holmes immortal? Why do people in this hectic technological age still thrill to the hansom cab ride through a thick Victorian London fog, knowing that once more 'the game is afoot'. One possible answer has been suggested by Vincent Starret in *The Private Life of Sherlock Holmes* (London, Nicholson and Watson, 1934): 'The Sherlockian elects to remain – as far as possible – in the predicament of Walter De La Mare's "Jim Jay who got stuck fast in yesterday." It is comforting in these troubled times to recall the old *Strand Magazine* of the turn of the century when Sherlock Holmes was adventuring, memorising, hounding and returning.' The Holmes stories exude an atmosphere that instantly transports us back to a far more leisurely world, and to a way of life we picture nostalgically, with a deepening envy as time passes.

The reason for Holmes's continuing popularity is not a simple one, but I believe that the cinema has played a major part in perpetuating and enhancing the Holmes legend, and it is the film career of the world's most famous consulting detective that I intend to examine in this book. But first I feel it is only fair to look at the original creator of the man who was to turn criminology into an exact science.

CONAN DOYLE

Sir Arthur Conan Doyle, the creator of Sherlock Holmes, said this about the genesis of his character on a gramophone recording shortly before his death:

> I was educated in a very severe and critical school of medical thought especially coming under the influence of Doctor Bell of Edinburgh who had the most remarkable powers of observation. He prided himself that when he looked at a patient he could tell not only their disease, but very often their occupation and place of residence. Reading some detective stories I was struck by the fact that their results were obtained in nearly every case by chance. I thought I would try my hand at writing a story in which the hero would treat crime as Doctor Bell treated disease and where science would take the place of chance.

The result was the first Sherlock Holmes novel, *A Study in Scarlet*, which appeared in *Beeton's Christmas Annual* in 1887. The editor of *Lippincott's Magazine* read the story and thought highly enough of it to invite Conan Doyle to write another story about Sherlock Holmes. This became *The Sign of Four* (originally titled *The Sign of the Four*) which was published in 1890.

Neither of these stories excited much interest. Then in the summer of 1891 the *Strand Magazine* published a Holmes short story, *A Scandal in Bohemia*, and almost immediately the imagination of the reading public was captured by the figure of Sherlock Holmes, and there was a demand for more stories. Conan Doyle agreed to write another five stories; after that he planned to devote himself to the historical romances which he valued more highly.

But as the popularity of the Holmes adventures grew, the *Strand* urged their creator to continue. Conan Doyle eventually relented when offered the sum of £1000 for a dozen stories.

Silver Blaze, the first story in the new series, appeared in the *Strand* in December 1892 and the twelve were published in book form in 1894 as *The Memoirs of Sherlock Holmes*. At this time the author wrote to his mother about his detective hero, 'he takes my mind from better things'. Conan Doyle was determined to do away with his creation and in *The Final Problem* which appeared in the *Strand* in 1893, he left little doubt that Holmes had perished under the Reichenbach Falls in Switzerland locked in a death grapple with his arch-enemy Professor Moriarty.

It seemed the world had seen the last of the man whom Dr Watson regarded as, 'the best and wisest man whom I have ever known'. The reading public were aghast. There was a national outcry; young city men took to wearing crepe 'weepers' in their top hats, many protests were made to the author who remained adamant: 'Thank God, I've killed the brute.'

For years Conan Doyle disregarded all pleas to resurrect Holmes, but in 1902 when he heard a friend's account of some legends of Dartmoor he conceived a mystery story about a family haunted by a spectral hound and decided to present it as an earlier adventure from Holmes's casebook. *The Hound of the Baskervilles* appeared in the *Strand* in 1901 and 1902 and was published in book form in the latter year. Of the Holmes novels this is perhaps the most successful, although the problem itself is not difficult to solve and the identity of the murderer is revealed two thirds of the way through. The dramatic tension of *The Hound of the Baskervilles* is maintained in the way in which Conan Doyle makes the reader experience the terrors and loneliness of the Devon moors, showing the disturbed feelings of the sober doctor who discovers beside the body of Sir Charles Baskerville 'the footprints of a gigantic hound'. It is its macabre appeal that has made it the most filmed of all the Holmes stories.

Conan Doyle was knighted in 1902 and it was felt – not entirely without reason – to be due as much to the reappearance of Holmes in *The Hound of the Baskervilles* as to the author's public service in rallying world opinion on British conduct during the Boer War.

Though the mortal remains of Holmes himself were still supposed to be at the bottom of the Reichenbach Falls, the publication of the Dartmoor adventure had revived hopes in the minds of publishers and readers alike that Holmes might make a permanent reappearance. Their hopes were realised in 1903 when Conan Doyle reluctantly agreed to bring his detective back to life. He did so in the story *The Empty House* which began the new series later to be grouped under the title *The Return of Sherlock Holmes*.

The Empty House contained details of the detective's miraculous escape from the duel with Moriarty at Reichenbach, and of his reunion with the ever faithful Watson and their reinstatement in their old Baker Street chambers which Watson had kept on in Holmes's absence.

There was a rush to obtain copies of the *Strand* which contained this story. By lunchtime on the day of publication long queues had formed outside the publisher's offices in Southampton Street. The printing presses had to be kept going night and day to keep pace with the demand and, according to eye-witnesses, 'the scenes at the railway bookstalls were worse . . . than a bargain sale'.

From this point on the canon continued uninterrupted until 1927 when Conan Doyle penned the final entry in the Holmes saga, *Shoscombe Old Place*.

In the introduction to the omnibus edition of the four long Holmes stories published in 1927, two years before his death, Doyle wrote: 'I trust that the younger public may find these romances of interest and that here and there one of the older generation may recapture an ancient thrill.'

Behind the lean figure of Holmes, throughout his career, there is the ampler one of his faithful chronicler Dr Watson. Watson, who is as necessary to the Holmes legend as the detective himself, was described by Desmond MacCarthy as the most representative Englishman of his period. Watson saw military service in Afghanistan and is always ready to arm himself with his service revolver when Holmes considers the danger warrants it. He is always available, ready to neglect his health, his wife, his practice or his safety at the call of duty. 'Come at once – if convenient – if inconvenient come all the same' wired Holmes peremptorily in a famous telegram. His loyalty to Holmes is unquestionable and, at times, touching. Moreover he accepts the brilliance of Holmes without trying to emulate him: 'I trust I am not more dense than my neighbours'. Holmes says of him: 'It may be you are not yourself luminous, but you are a conductor of light.' This succinctly sums up their relationship in which Watson is the foil to Holmes, the hero.

Another character inextricably caught up in the Holmes legend is Professor James Moriarty, 'the Napoleon of crime'. This evil genius, who is to be found in well over half the Holmes films, is only actually featured in two of the sixty stories that make up the Conan Doyle canon. But his character, like that of Holmes, has captured the imagination of the public and the film-makers. As Holmes tells Watson in *The Final Problem*:

> He is the organiser of half that is evil and nearly all that is undetected in this great city. He has a brain of the first order. He sits motionless like a spider in the centre of its web, but that web has a thousand radiations and he knows well every quiver of them.

Here then Conan Doyle created a villain of sufficient merit to challenge the great detective on the same intellectual plane, and the battle of wits between these two protagonists has provided the core of many Holmes films.

After this short consideration of two of the Baker Street satellites, I will now take a closer look at the star.

'YOU KNOW MY METHODS'

Sherlock Holmes emerges from the Conan Doyle canon as a cerebral animal: 'I cannot live without brainwork, what else is there to live for?' His cognitive pursuits seem to cover many areas: 'He spoke on a quick succession of subjects – on miracle plays, on mediaeval pottery, on Stradivarius violins, on the Buddhism of Ceylon and on the warships of the future – handling each as though he had made a special study of it.'

If a man is proclaimed as superior to others, his superiority must be demonstrated. It is a weakness in a number of the Holmes films that his genius is announced but not proved. But in the canon, Doyle reveals gradually the astounding extent of Holmes's knowledge, his monographs on 140 different varieties of pipe, cigar and cigarette tobaccos, on the ear, on the Polyphonic Motets of Lassus, his analysis of 160 ciphers, his ability to distinguish the type of any newspaper at a glance.

Doyle recognised the need for Holmes to be a man immune from ordinary human weaknesses and feelings. Holmes therefore rejects passion, indeed any strong feelings towards women. He does admire Irene Adler – 'she is always the woman' – but only, we are assured, because she proved his equal in quickness of wit and decisiveness of action.

Stamford, the man who introduces Watson to Holmes, says of him: '[he] is a little too scientific for my tastes – it approaches to cold bloodedness'. It is as a cool, detached reasoner that Holmes is found to be most fascinating. He deliberated on this trait in *The Sign of Four*: 'Detection is, or ought to be an exact science, and should be treated in the same cold and unemotional manner.'

Observation and deduction are his methods. Given a battered old felt hat, of which Watson can make nothing, Holmes is able to deduce that the owner is highly intellectual, was fairly well-to-do but is now poor and has been deteriorating, probably under the influence of drink. This may account for the obvious fact that his wife has ceased to love him.

But Holmes is not an armchair academic playing detective, he is very much a man of action, and it is through this aspect of the man that the potency of the Holmes stories reaches its full power: the call in the night; the hansom cab ride through the gaslit streets into danger. As Watson puts it: 'It was indeed like old times when at that hour I found myself beside him in a hansom, my revolver in my pocket and the thrill of adventure in my heart.'

Holmes's addiction to cocaine (a seven per cent solution), mentioned quite fully in *The Sign of Four* but not referred to in most of the other stories, has received far more attention from the film world than is warranted. Holmes's need of the drug does not spring from any hedonistic desire, but simply from a need to counteract the boredom of inactivity; although some screenwriters appear to have been determined to present Holmes as an addict.

One of Holmes's many facets exploited by the cinema was his ability to adopt a disguise. As Athenely Jones of Scotland Yard noted in *The Sign of Four*: 'You would have made an actor and a rare one'.

One of the essential Sherlockian props is the Stradivarius violin with which Holmes was able to escape 'from this weary, workaday world by the side door of music': 'Hand me my violin and let us try to forget for half an hour the miserable weather, and the still more miserable ways of our fellow-men.'

Principal among the things that spring to mind when considering Sherlock Holmes are the way he keeps saying 'Elementary, my dear Watson' and the number of times he puffs on his meerschaum pipe. But according to the Doyle canon they are both inaccurate. Holmes often says the word 'Elementary' in

Sherlock Holmes and Dr Watson in traditional gear as portrayed by Sidney Paget.

the sixty stories, and he often says 'My dear Watson', but never the two together. As for the meerschaum pipe – that was really started by the actor William Gillette who played the part of Holmes on Broadway. It is not referred to in the original.

What then of the famous deerstalker? Again this is never specifically referred to in the original stories – the nearest Doyle got to it is the mention of Holmes's 'close fitting cloth cap'. It was from this description first mentioned in *Silver Blaze* that the illustrator Sidney Paget, who liked to wear a deer-stalker when in the country, placed this headgear on Holmes – the two having been synonymous in the public mind ever since.

How did Doyle picture his hero? Physical description is in fact sparse but we do get some pointers, particularly in *A Study in Scarlet*:

> His very person and appearance were such as to strike the attention of the most casual observer. In height he was rather over six feet, and so excessively lean that he seemed to be considerably taller. His eyes were sharp and piercing and his thin hawk-like nose gave his whole expression an air of alertness and decision. His chin, too, had the prominence and squareness, which mark the man of determination.

The very stylisation of this portrait draws our attention to the essential qualities of the consulting detective: his energy and the acuteness of his senses. But this certainly left something to the imagination of his illustrator Sidney Paget who used his brother Walter as the model for Holmes. And it was from Paget's drawings that the definitive image of Sherlock Holmes emerged.

This then is the Sherlock Holmes of Conan Doyle's imagination. We now move on to see how the cinema has contributed to this portrait to build a complete personality with an independent existence of its own.

Chapter 2

The Silent Sherlock

IN 1903, the same year that he was making a reappearance on the literary scene in *The Empty House*, Sherlock Holmes made his début on the screen in an American film made by the American Mutoscope and Bioscope Company entitled *Sherlock Holmes Baffled*. The audiences first seeing the film may also have been baffled, for the film bore no recognisable plot and seems to be little more than a series of tableaux of a melodramatic nature without any real continuity. Since the American Mutoscope and Bioscope Co did not begin to use recognisable actors until much later, it is most probable that Holmes was played by the studio employee who most resembled the traditional image of the detective.

Holmes's second screen exploit also originated from an American studio. The film, a Vitagraph production of 1905, bore two titles: *Held for a Ransom* and *The Adventures of Sherlock Holmes*. This film was a great improvement on the previous one, for it had a recognisable story line, but it is too early a film to be regarded as a valuable contribution to the Holmes picture gallery.

Three years later the Crescent company, one of a number of rapidly proliferating, but generally short lived American independent film companies, came up with *Sherlock Holmes and the Great Murder Mystery*. The plot appears to have been inspired by Edgar Allan Poe's *Murder in the Rue Morgue* and involved murder by a gorilla!

On 2 May 1908 *Moving Picture World* reviewed a short Italian film,

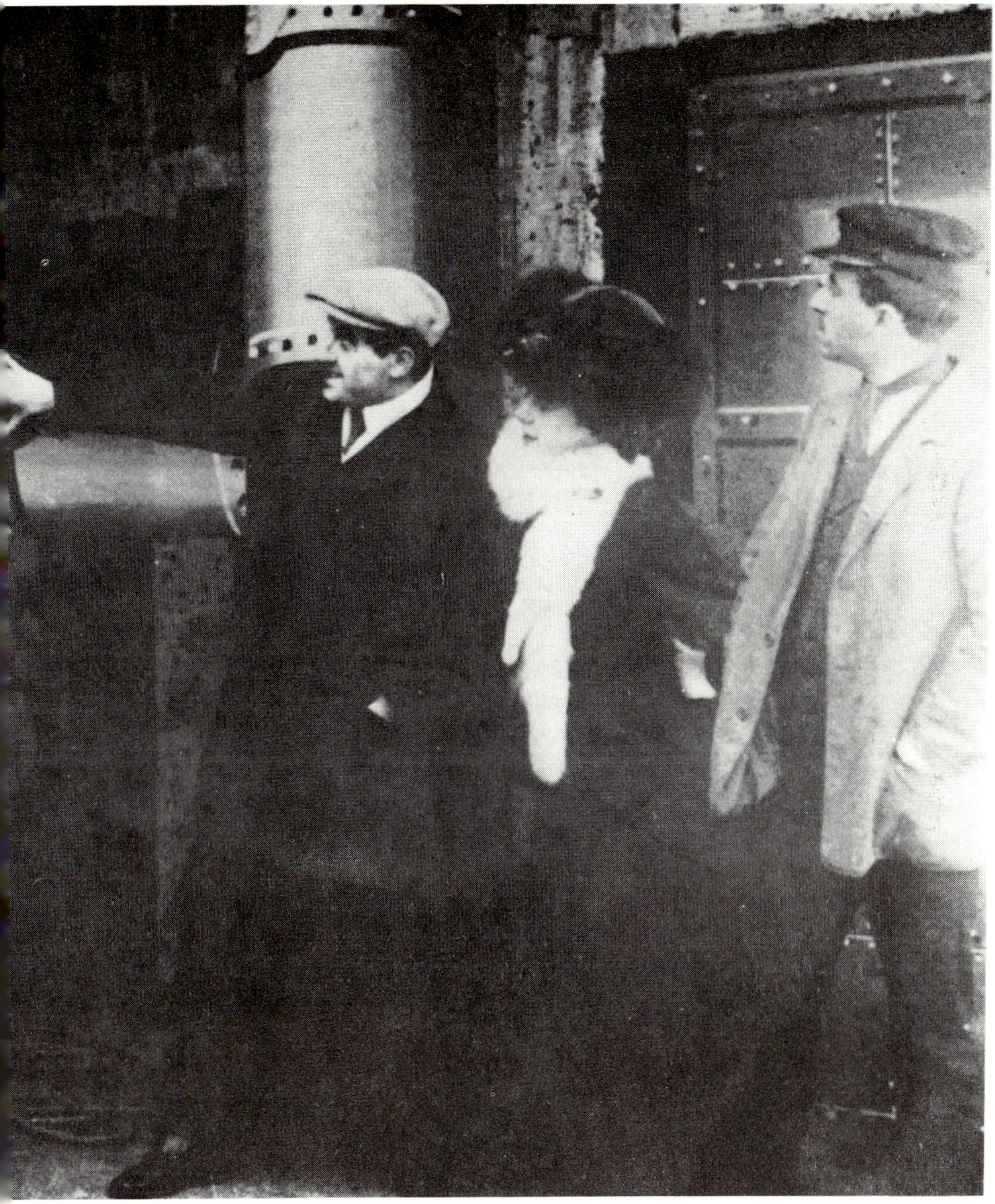

Sherlock Holmes (Viggo Larsen) trussed by the villains in *Sherlock Holmes in the Gas Cellar* (1908). *Nordisk*

Rival Sherlock Holmes released by Ambrosio, as follows: 'A pictorial detective story of merit with many lightning changes of disguise by the detective in his pursuit of the lawbreakers. Exciting scenes and physical encounters are numerous. A sensational subject of superb dramatic effect, without any objectionable features.' *Moving Picture World*'s review did not make clear whether the title referred to Holmes himself or to a detective meant to be Holmes's rival.

Sherlock Holmes was still being ignored as a screen subject by the British film companies in 1908 when the Nordisk Company of Denmark embarked on a whole series of Holmes films directed by Forrect Holger-Madsen who also played the lead, while Watson was played by Alwin Neuss. Unfortunately information concerning these films is scarce for there are no existing copies of the twelve films made in the series. However, records indicate that the films had well staged physical action, a good deal of exterior shooting, and an authentic Holmesian atmosphere.

Apart from the utilisation of Professor Moriarty as Holmes's antagonist in some of the films, others brought him face to face with Raffles, the debonair cracksman hero created by E.W. Hornung. Presumably this literary contemporary was depicted more in a criminal than in an heroic light. Film makers in those days were none too scrupulous about recognising the still vague copyright laws, or about using a character's name and changing his image entirely. The Danish series of one-reelers was made over a three year period.

Germany made two Holmes films in 1910 and like the Scandinavian efforts they mixed in another literary character. This time Edgar Allan Poe's Arsene Lupin replaced Moriarty as Holmes's sparring partner.

By 1910 the real potential of Holmes as a film character seems to have been realised by most film making nations except, ironically, the British. Surprisingly, Sexton Blake a juvenile carbon copy of Holmes featured in the *Union Jack Weekly*, a popular comic of the day, appeared in British films long before Holmes. In 1908 Douglas Carlile directed and played the title role in *Sexton Blake*. The film must have been reasonably successful for it spawned two sequels: *The Jewel Thieves Run to Earth by Sexton Blake* and *Sexton Blake v Baron Kettler*.

In 1911 the British produced *A Case for Sherlock Holmes* but the plot involves a dog routing a gang of crooks and the Baker Street detective does not make an appearance.

The first authentic entry in the Sherlock Holmes stakes to come from the British stables was in fact a series of Anglo-French two-reelers made in 1912. Allegedly Conan Doyle was personally involved in their production. The films were directed by Frenchman Georges Treville who also played Holmes; a Mr Moyse played Watson. The titles (for a complete list see the filmography) suggest that the films adhered closely to the Doyle canon for their plots. The last film in the series, *The Copper Beeches*, has the distinction of being the earliest known extant Holmes film, although now it is too battered and delicate to risk projection.

The French made the first film versions of *A Study in Scarlet* and *The Hound of the Baskervilles* in 1914-15 before abandoning the essentially British Holmes to concentrate on their own native mystery specialists, Fantomas and Judex.

The same year as the French *A Study in Scarlet* the British produced a version of the same story and two years after this six-reeler Holmes feature there came another: *The Valley of Fear*. Both these films were produced by G.B. Samuelson, a noted British pioneer whose work was well above the usual, admittedly not very high, standards. Production expansion had been curtailed by the outbreak of war.

During the war comedy films were for obvious reasons more popular and as a result of this the two Holmes features were not as well received as they

A rare still from one of the earliest Sherlock Holmes movies *The Murder in Baker Street.* **The great detective is played by Alwin Neuss (1908-12).** *Nordisk*

might have been. But the character of Holmes was used by comedy film makers in many Sherlockian parodies during the war years. One of the prolific *Pimple* films which featured a likeable buffoon in various humorous situations was entitled *Pimple's Case of Johnny Walker*. Fred Evans appeared in the film as Sherlock Pimple. He also played in another Sherlockian parody in 1915, *A Study in Skarlit*, which featured a comical battle of wits between Sherlokz Holmz and Professor Moratorium. In 1916 a character called Sherlock Blake appeared in a Billy Mersen comedy, *The Terrible Tec*.

In Germany in 1917 Richard Oswald, a prolific but rather stodgy and unimaginative director made *The Hound of the Baskervilles*. Oswald, who had a penchant for remaking his big commercial hits, repeated *The Hound* in 1929, surprisingly still as a silent feature, with Carlyle Blackwell singularly miscast as Holmes.

With the end of the First World War, the British audiences were once again ready to accept the sort of dramas which had fallen out of favour during

James Bragington, a suitably gaunt looking Sherlock Holmes, examines the corpse in a scene from *A Study in Scarlet* (1914). *Samuelson*

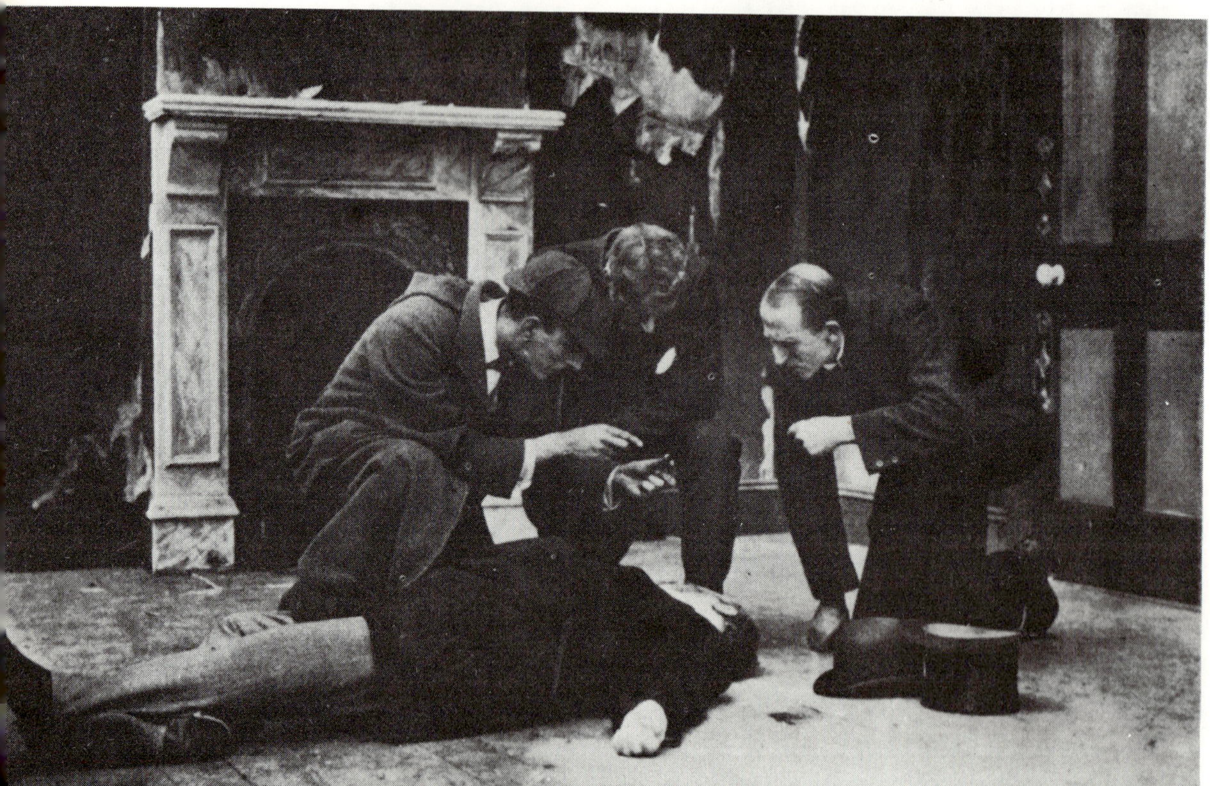

the years of conflict. Early in 1921 there appeared the first serious all-British series of Holmes films. *The Adventures of Sherlock Holmes* numbered fifteen in all (for a complete list of titles see the filmography) and were directed by Maurice Elvey who also had a hand in the screenplays. The plots, except for some slight modernisations, were faithful to the original Conan Doyle stories.

These films featured Eille Norwood as Holmes. Just as Gillette *was* Sherlock Holmes to the theatre audiences of his generation, so Eille Norwood was to the moviegoers of the twenties. When the Stoll company decided to produce the film series, Norwood was invited to play the leading role. According to the *Leader* of 23 August 1947, at first director Maurice Elvey disagreed with Norwood's interpretation of Holmes, but the actor was insistent. 'Let's film your way first, then mine', he suggested. So they took several shots of each scene and next day went to the studio theatre to see their first day's work on the screen. Elvey agreed that Norwood was right.

Studying the first script at home, Norwood had been horrified to read the words: 'Enter Sherlock Holmes in a white beard.' He protested strongly. 'But Holmes would never have done that,' he said. It was obvious that the film executives had little idea what Holmes would have done, and when Norwood outlined his plans for disguises, they were dubious. Jeffrey Bernard, production chief of Stolls, told him he would never be able to disguise his height and appearance.

The next day Bernard noticed a small taxi driver standing on the studio set and, as visitors were not allowed in the studios, he sent someone to remove him. The taxi driver insisted, in the best Cockney, that his taxi was outside and that he was only watching. For several minutes technicians argued with him then he drew himself up to his full height and revealed himself as Eille Norwood.

Norwood said that he modelled his performance on Sidney Paget's illustrations, and certainly he did possess a fiercely cut profile and magnetic eyes. So popular became Norwood, that he played Holmes on stage in 1923 in a play called *The Return of Sherlock Holmes*. A contemporary reviewer stated: 'Mr Eille Norwood's performance as Holmes seemed to me admirable.' Doyle himself wrote of Norwood: 'He has that rare quality which can only be described as glamour which compels you to watch an actor eagerly when he is doing nothing. He has a brooding eye which excites expectation and he has a quite unrivalled power of disguise.'

In the first fifteen films Watson was played by Hubert Willis who unfortunately bore a resemblance to Norwood, and viewing the faded films today it is sometimes difficult to distinguish which actor is which. Miri d'Esterre played Mrs Hudson the housekeeper and Arthur Bell played Inspector Lestrade.

Later in 1921 the same team brought the first British version of *The Hound of the Baskervilles* to the screen. Although Maurice Elvey was an experienced film-maker who turned out films with astonishing regularity between

Above: Sherlock Holmes (Eille Norwood) alerts Sir Henry Baskerville (Rex McDougall) to some important features of a family portrait. A scene from *The Hound of the Baskervilles* (1921). *Stoll*

Left: The moor at sunset. Eille Norwood in *The Hound of the Baskervilles* (1921). *Stoll*

Below: Eille Norwood having a quick lurk in *The Hound of the Baskervilles* (1921). *Stoll*

1913 and 1957, tackling everything from historical pageantry and slapstick to Dickens, war films and science fiction, he was not an imaginative enough director to evoke moods, to create atmospheres or suggest menace from a script that did not tell him how. *The Hound of the Baskervilles* of all films needs mood more than it needs logic or action, and mood is one thing this version consistently lacks.

Baskerville Hall, never seen in relation to its supposedly bleak surroundings, looks exactly like what it probably was – a London suburban town house, belonging to someone of considerable but not spectacular wealth. The forays onto Grimpen Mire suggest sparse parkland or possibly early morning filming on Hampstead Heath, but one never has the sense of desolation, of sweeping moorland and treacherous quagmire. Undoubtedly aware of the shortcomings of exteriors, Elvey keeps most of his action indoors, thus reducing the effectiveness of this eerie tale. The result is a stodgy and lack-lustre production. There is however one touch of showmanship: the hound was tinted or handpainted with a luminous glow, so that its infrequent appearances do carry a token shock value.

Sherlock Holmes (John Barrymore) comes face to face with his arch enemy, Moriarty (Gustav von Seyffertitz), in *Sherlock Holmes* (1922). (*Goldwyn Pictures*)

Interestingly enough, Elvey made a Spanish style romantic drama the same year *The Fruitful Vine* in which the lead was played by Basil Rathbone whose name was later to become indissolubly linked with that of Sherlock Holmes.

Although *Adventures of Sherlock Holmes* and *The Hound of the Baskervilles* were not a marked success, Eille Norwood was, and as a result another fifteen two-reelers (for a complete list of titles see the filmography) were produced in 1922. Called *Further Adventures of Sherlock Holmes,* they were directed by George Ridgewell.

The first really elaborate Holmes film was produced in America in 1922 by Samuel Goldwyn, and had as its basis the William Gillette play. John Barrymore merged his famous profile with that of the famous detective to present a youthful and very individualistic Holmes. Despite the fact that *Sherlock Holmes* was criticised for its hokum, for being more a Barrymore than a Holmes film, it was immensely popular. The film was exquisitely lit and had a generous budget which allowed extensive authentic location shooting in London.

Location shooting in London for Goldwyn's 1922 *Sherlock Holmes.*

Gustav von Seyffertitz played a not only mentally but also physically corrupt Moriarty: a far more grotesque creation than the suave villain of Conan Doyle's imagination. Both he and Barrymore assumed several disguises in the course of the picture and in one climactic scene, Holmes disguised as Moriarty comes face to face with the real Moriarty. The film, directed by Albert Parker, had a large cast which included Roland Young as Dr Watson, William Powell in his movie debut as a villain, and Carol Dempster as Alice Faulkner who at the film's end is all set to marry Holmes.

It has been suggested that, although there may have been legal reasons, the mediocrity of so many of the earlier Holmes films was the deciding factor in releasing the film in Britain under the title of *Moriarty*.

Back in Britain in 1923 yet another series of fifteen two-reelers were produced (for a complete list of titles see the filmography). This time they were called *The Last Adventures of Sherlock Holmes*. George Ridgewell once more directed Eille Norwood as Holmes and Hubert Willis as Watson, while Tom Beaumont doubled as Inspectors Lestrade and Gregory in various films.

These films did not bring about the last adventures of Eille Norwood's Holmes for he appeared later in the same year in a tame six-reel version of *The Sign of Four*. Hubert Willis was replaced by Arthur Cullin as Watson. This was the last Holmes film that Norwood made and *The Sign of Four* provided the swan-song of the silent Sherlock in Britain.

Sherlock Holmes (Eille Norwood) gets the bird in *The Blue Carbuncle* (1923). *Stoll*

Above: Sherlock Holmes (Eille Norwood, left) makes enquiries in *The Disappearance of Lady Frances Carfax* (1923). *Stoll*

Below: Sherlock Holmes (Eille Norwood) holds the sinister snake in the dénouement of the 1923 version of *The Speckled Band. Stoll*

Chapter 3

A Theatrical Diversion

THE very first American feature-length Holmes film was made in 1916. Entitled *Sherlock Holmes*, it was based on the play written as a vehicle for himself by William Gillette who had been playing the role on stage for some seventeen years. He was therefore the logical choice to star in the film version.

At this point it would be appropriate to relate the history of the play *Sherlock Holmes*. Four years after Conan Doyle had murdered his detective creation, the desire to write a really successful play led his thoughts again to Holmes and he sent a Sherlock Holmes play to Herbert Beerbohm Tree. Characteristically, Tree asked that the central character be rewritten to make it more like Beerbohm Tree than Sherlock Holmes. Doyle was understandably reluctant to do this and rapidly lost interest. The whole project might have been dropped altogether, but Conan Doyle's literary agent sent the play to American impresario Charles Frohman in New York and Frohman accepted it. Again rewriting was demanded, this time by William Gillette who was anxious to play the lead. Conan Doyle was so indifferent to the whole project by this time that when he received a telegram from Gillette asking for permission to 'marry Holmes', he replied: 'You may marry or murder or do what you like with him.'

So in the autumn of 1899 William Gillette arrived in England with his version of the play to gain Conan Doyle's approval. The meeting between the two men, one the creator of probably the world's greatest fictional detective, the other a man destined to become one of the greatest portrayers of that character, must have been electric. John Dickson Carr records the episode in his excellent biography, *The Life of Sir Arthur Conan Doyle* (John Murray, 1949):

> At the railway station, some distance from Undershaw, he [Conan Doyle] waited in the two-horse landau. He had never seen William Gillette, even in a photograph. He knew nothing about Gillette except the latter's high reputation as an actor. The London train, its green painted carriages then numbered for first and second class clattered to a stop. And out of it, in a long grey cape, stepped the living image of Sherlock Holmes.
>
> Not even Sidney Paget had done it so well in a drawing. The clear cut features, the deep set eyes looked out under a deerstalker cap; even Gillette's age, the middle forties, was right. Conan Doyle, in the landau, contemplated him open-mouthed. It is not recorded that the horses shied; but this was the general effect.

Conan Doyle thought Gillette's adaptation of his original 'had turned it into a fine play' and subsequently *Sherlock Holmes* opened in New York in November 1899 and ran for 236 performances.

The drama was described as an hitherto unpublished case in the career of the great detective and showed his connection with the 'strange case of Miss Faulkner'. However the plot relied heavily on two of Conan Doyle's short stories, *A Scandal in Bohemia* and *The Final Problem* and the play is littered with Sherlockian quotations from other stories. The encounter between Moriarty and Holmes is lifted virtually intact from the canon: 'All I have to say has already crossed your mind,' warns Moriarty; 'Then possibly my answer has crossed yours,' retorts Holmes.

The most striking innovation and the most jarring note struck in the play is Holmes's romance. A love interest is unthinkable to the Sherlockian purist, for as Holmes says to Watson in *The Sign of Four*: 'Love is an emotional thing and whatever is emotional is opposed to that true cold reason which I place above all things. I should never marry myself lest I bias my judgement.'

It is hard to reconcile this Holmes with the one in Gillette's play who finally surrenders to the charms of Alice Faulkner:

> I suppose – indeed I know – that I love you. I love you. But I know as well what I am – and what you are – I know that no such person as I should ever dream of being part of your sweet life. It would be a crime for me to think of such a thing. There is every reason –

William Gillette in the gas chamber scene from the play *Sherlock Holmes. The Stanley MacKenzie Collection*

But Alice is not interested in reasons. She gently places her right hand on Holmes's breast and is shortly resting in his arms. And so the curtain falls.

After the success of this 'absurd, preposterous and thoroughly delightful melodrama' in New York, Gillette toured with it and brought it to London in 1901 where it ran at the Lyceum Theatre for another 216 performances.

The drama critic of the *Daily Telegraph* reported after opening night: 'The performance of the American actor is in many respects interesting though it is hardly great. In fact there is a certain stiffness of monotony about it . . .' The *Times* critic was hardly more complimentary: 'It would be a shame to tell the story, even if we completely understood it.'

Despite the cool reception from the press both Gillette and the play were even more successful in England than in America. It is interesting to note that young Charlie Chaplin played the page boy, Billy, during the play's London run.

Like several other actors Gillette made a career out of playing Holmes and appeared in revivals of this play in 1905, 1906, 1910 and 1915. It was in 1916 that Gillette at the age of sixty-one filmed *Sherlock Holmes* with a screenplay by H.S. Sheldon. At this time many stage personalities were being brought to Hollywood to re-create their famous theatrical roles and, incidentally, to bring a little prestige and respectability to what was still considered a bastard art.

The Essanay production of *Sherlock Holmes*, directed by Arthur Berthelet, must have been a frustrating vehicle for Holmes's fans: Gillette, at this time the definitive interpreter of Holmes, was recreating his finest role, but robbed of words which are so important to the Holmes persona. Of course this failing is common to all the Holmes films of the silent era. A comment cannot be made on the quality of this film as it is no longer extant, but other films of the same period recording famous stage performances are rather primitive efforts in which one never sees a close up of the actor but is presented instead with a series of badly framed long shots.

A contemporary reviewer wrote of *Sherlock Holmes*:

> The film version follows very closely on the lines of the stage play and the producer has made no attempt to bring the story up to date. The modern motorcar without which the present day crook could not carry on his work has not been allowed to supersede the hansom cab of fifteen years ago.
>
> The story of Alice Faulkner and the papers she holds relating to some Prince of Royal Blood, the blackmailer Larrabee and the great criminal Moriarty, Sherlock Holmes, and Dr Watson have become such familiar

William Gillette in his famous Sherlock Holmes dressing-gown. *The Stanley MacKenzie Collection*

William Gillette

> figures as to almost lose the charm of novelty which every participant in detective drama should be called upon to supply. Without the dialogue some of the situations seem to misfire.
>
> Mr Gillette retains the quaint eccentricities of dress he adopted when the play was first performed, which includes a brocaded dressing-gown, velvet collar and cuffs and of course a deerstalker. Mr Gillette has a distinctive personality and holds the attention by his own magnetism whenever he appears on the screen. It is rather curious to note that an actor who has made his reputation to so great an extent by the quietness and restraint of his methods should appear a little hurried and spasmodic when seen through the medium of the camera, though this in no way deprives the character of his effectiveness.

Gillette revived the play again in 1923 and then retired. But in 1929 at the age of 74 he emerged from retirement and began an astonishing Farewell Tour of the United States. Conan Doyle lived just long enough to congratulate the aging Gillette:

> May I add a word to those which are addressed to you on the occasion of your return to the stage. That this return should be in *Sherlock Holmes* is of course a source of personal gratification. My only complaint being that you make the poor hero of the anaemic printed page a very limp object as compared with the glamour of your own personality which you infuse into his stage presentment.

Praise indeed!

So overwhelming was Gillette's reception on the tour that it was three seasons later, in May 1932, before he completed it. Even then he had not quite finished with the play, he performed it for the last time for CBS in a radio broadcast in 1935, two years before he died. All that has survived of his years playing Sherlock Holmes is a scrap of dialogue from the radio play: an unworthy legacy from a great career. Booth Tarkington expressed the feelings of many of Gillette's admirers when he said that he would rather see the actor play Sherlock Holmes than be a child again on Christmas morning.

At the end of Gillette's final tour the play faded from view, but it surfaced for a month at Birmingham Rep in 1952 (with Alfred Burke as Holmes) and in BBC Radio's Saturday Night Theatre in 1954 where it had the starry cast of John Gielgud as Holmes, Ralph Richardson as Watson and Orson Welles as Moriarty. This production was given the full Victorian melodrama treatment including audience cheers, boos and hisses.

The play was recently successfully revived by the Royal Shakespeare Company in 1974 when it received excellent reviews in which one critic referred to John Wood's performance as Holmes as 'a great acting achievement'. The play subsequently went to Broadway where it was performed to packed houses.

The success of the play, without the persona of Gillette emphasises what a bad judge the reviewer of the New York *Tribune* was in 1899 when he wrote of *Sherlock Holmes*: 'The play has no lasting value whatever.'

Chapter 4

Holmes Talks!

IN the middle twenties, the movie box office sagged. Something seemed to have gone wrong; except for the big pictures, the audiences were staying at home in ever increasing numbers. The Warner Brothers, in an attempt to revive the interest in movies and their own failing fortunes, gambled all they had on Vitaphone, a sound picture device developed by the engineers and technicians of the Bell Telephone Company. In 1927 after a few Vitaphone 'shorts' which involved adding sound-track music to otherwise silent films, they came up with *The Jazz Singer* starring Al Jolson. *The Jazz Singer* was a mediocre silent with a familiar plot and mostly told its story with titles, but it did contain three Jolson songs and a snatch of dialogue. That was enough. Once it was released in October 1927 the revolution was underway.

It was not until the advent of talking pictures that the cinema could attempt to do full justice to the Holmes legend. Sherlock Holmes, a verbal animal, needs a sound-track to give his brilliant deductions credence and potency. Reading captions of 'Elementary my dear Watson, the game is afoot', hardly has the same power and efficacy as the spoken word. Some of the silent films had been able to capture the mood and even present the action of the Holmes stories effectively, but their inevitable silence had made it impossible for them to furnish the cinema audiences with a fully rounded portrait of the famous sleuth.

When sound movies became a viable product, most big companies jumped on the bandwagon. There was at this time a shortage of screenwriters who could deal effectively with dialogue: what looks fine on a caption usually sounds trite or even stupid as spoken dialogue. So apart from a wealth of virtually plotless musicals, the film makers turned to the works of literature for their material where the dialogue was already written and needed merely to be condensed and rearranged. Therefore Sherlock Holmes was considered a natural for the talkies.

It was in the very early sound days of 1929, that the first talking Holmes appeared on the screen. He was played by Clive Brook, a British actor often seen in 'gentleman' or 'cad' roles. Brook portrayed Holmes with just the right amount of detachment, but it was a characteristic of his acting style to be stiffly formal – so much so that one critic, seeing him playing the romantic lead in *The Laughing Lady* (1930), pretended to mistake him for the butler. As a result of this stiffness, his Holmes at times appeared priggish and humourless. Nevertheless Brook was physically right for the part and had great screen presence. He emerges as perhaps the most interesting and effective Holmes up to that date.

The 1929 film was entitled *The Return of Sherlock Holmes*, although it was never revealed where he had been. It was an American production for Paramount release, shot, according to Brook, very quickly and cheaply in a small cramped studio in midtown Manhattan, and on a sea trip from England to New York. The film was limited in action, most of it taking place aboard an ocean liner, but the concentration on talk was typical of the films of the early sound days which exploited dialogue and sound rather than action.

As well as being the first sound Holmes, *The Return of Sherlock Holmes* was also the first film in which the detective was updated and presented as a contemporary character, and this seemed to increase his fascination for the cinema audiences. The plot was original, gracing Watson with a daughter and bore no resemblance to any of the Conan Doyle stories.

Holmes is attending the wedding of Roger Longmore to Mary, Watson's daughter, when Roger's father, Captain Longmore, is found murdered in his study. Holmes suspects poison after finding a trick cigarette case with a poisoned needle which is brought into play when the opening spring is pressed.

Meanwhile Roger disappears and, acting on a few slender clues, Holmes rushes off to Cherbourg with Watson and Mary where they catch a liner for America. Holmes suspects the ship's doctor and with the aid of various disguises, one of which is that of a German musician who performs conjuring tricks, he discovers Roger is on board. Holmes eventually comes face to face with his arch-enemy Professor Moriarty (played by Harry T. Morey), and one of the highlights of the film is the scene where Moriarty in disguise entertains Holmes to dinner, only to be finally unmasked. Rather than be taken alive, Moriarty commits suicide.

There were some colourful gimmicks used, such as Holmes's rather unnecessarily elaborate procedure of daubing the heels of Dr Watson's shoes with phosphorus so as to provide an illuminated track to Moriarty's cabin.

Watson was portrayed as a bumbling fatuous character by H. Reeves Smith who appeared noticeably older than Holmes. Despite Brook's reputedly excellent diction a contemporary review of the film comments that although in general the sound was good, the star's voice did not register as well as the others.

Later in the same year Clive Brook made a second appearance as Holmes in *Paramount on Parade* an all-star musical revue. He appeared as the detective

Sherlock Holmes (Clive Brook) ponders a problem while Moriarty (Harry T. Morey) prepares to pounce. A scene from *The Return of Sherlock Holmes* (1929). *Paramount*

Dr Watson (H. Reeves Smith), his wife Mary (Betty Lawford) and Sherlock Holmes (Clive Brook) in *The Return of Sherlock Holmes* (1929). *Paramount*

in a comedy sketch which also involved two of Paramount's other featured characters: Philo Vance (William Powell) and Fu Manchu (Warner Oland). It is of interest here only because it represents the one time that Sherlock Holmes has died on the screen.

Brook's final appearance as the man from Baker Street was in Fox's stylish 1932 production, titled simply *Sherlock Holmes*. The plot is based on Doyle by way of the Gillette play though oddly enough the official synopsis bears little similarity to the finished film written by Bertram Millhauser (who would reappear later as one of the perennial writers of Universal's Holmes series). Again Holmes was placed in a contemporary setting, so much so that the film showed him dealing with saloon bombings and other gangster methods which were contemporary phenomena in the States. Moriarty, beautifully played by Ernest Torrence, who delivered every line with a highly malignant, mock humility, is at the root of all the evil, of course.

Apparently drawing its main inspiration from Conan Doyle's *The Red-Headed League*, the film, directed by William K. Howard, is a finely polished and slick melodrama, although as a Holmes feature it is a little disappointing. The detective is given virtually no opportunity for his verbal reasoning and deductions, and the inevitable 'Elementary, my dear Watson' uttered as it is after moments of mundane observations seems to be used as a joke. Watson, played by Reginald Owen, makes only fleeting appearances and the interplay of the two characters is never established.

True Doyle devotees would also have been annoyed at the retention of the romance from the Gillette play, which involves Holmes falling in love with Alice Faulkner (played by Miriam Jordan).

Nevertheless the film is most enjoyable and has some beautifully composed and effectively lit shots. The opening is particularly effective: Moriarty is brought into court, sentenced to death and in his address to the jury promises that the rope that can hang him has not yet been made – and those responsible for his sentence, particularly Sherlock Holmes, will precede him in death.

The next scene shows Holmes dabbling with some elaborate electrical gadgetry in his laboratory, a set which was used in a number of science fiction films of the period. The detective is demonstrating a ray he has invented which the police will be able to use to demobilise the cars of escaping crooks. It is his parting gift to Scotland Yard and he gives a short speech about how the motor car has become a deadly weapon of crime.

Meanwhile back at the prison there is chaos. George Barnes's smoothly flowing camera follows the prison guards as they race down the grim corridors, and eventually along the walls of a cell block to a message scrawled on the wall: 'Tell Holmes I'm OUT'.

After this superb atmospheric opening there follows a highly efficient thriller with a plot which involves Moriarty's revenge and his plan to get Holmes to the gallows by forcing him into a murder. At one point Holmes is

Sherlock Holmes (Clive Brook) disguised as an old Lady in *Sherlock Holmes* (1932). *Fox*

Right: Reginald Owen, one of the least convincing Sherlock Holmes in *A Study in Scarlet* (1933). *Worldwide*

arrested, but he manages to use this setback to his own advantage. There are however some ludicrous moments, like the instance when Holmes is disguised as a prissy maiden aunt complete with a high-pitched grating voice. Holmes, as in many films, appears to be extraordinarily lucky in his disguises, for while moviegoers are not fooled for one minute, the villains are consistently deceived.

After an exciting climax featuring a bank robbery, it is understood that the immortal detective is going to settle down. Alice Faulkner has apparently succeeded in persuading Holmes to abandon his dangerous life to keep chickens. There can have been little doubt in the mind of the moviegoer that this retirement would not last, although Holmes was never again played by Clive Brook, whom one contemporary reviewer called 'a well nourished but otherwise engaging Holmes'.

Hollywood's next Holmes vehicle was the independently produced *A Study in Scarlet* (1933). Reginald Owen was promoted from his Watson role to that of the great sleuth himself. Owen has the distinction of being the only

actor to have played both Holmes and Watson, but being singularly miscast he remains the least effective Holmes of all. If Brook appeared well nourished, Owen was positively plump. One contemporary reviewer noted: 'Reginald Owen seems to have been cast for the chief role because he has an English accent rather than because he resembles the favourite detective of fiction.'

The film took nothing but the title from Doyle's novel. Instead it concerned the nefarious doings of a criminal organisation called the 'Scarlet Ring' and apart from an exceptionally strong cast for a small company like World-wide (Anna May Wong, Alan Vinehart, and Warburton Gamble as Watson) the verbose and tedious film had little to recommend it.

The German film makers renewed their interest in Holmes in the mid-thirties. In 1936 Carl Lamac directed *Der Hund von Baskervilles* with Pieter Voss, Alice Brandt and Fritz Rasp, and in 1937 Erich Engels directed *Die Grave Dame* with Hermann Speelman and Elizabeth Wendt. The latter, though a Holmes film, was not based on a Doyle work but a play by Muller Puzika called *The Deed of the Unknown.*

Lyn Harding as Dr Rylott and Raymond Massey as Sherlock Holmes in *The Speckled Band.* **Harding was later to play Moriarty twice to Arthur Wontner's Holmes** (1931). *British and Dominion*

In 1937 a German spoof was produced called *Der Mann Der Sherlock Holmes War*. In this film, Hans Albens the matinée idol and Heinz Ruhmann played two private detectives down on their luck who decide to pass themselves off as Holmes and Watson, and in so doing, solve the mystery of a stolen stamp. Throughout the film the two principals keep meeting an Englishman who bursts out laughing at each encounter. In the dénouement he is identified as Conan Doyle.

With the coming of sound, British studios also busied themselves with Holmes films. In 1929 Conan Doyle himself appeared in a fifteen minute talking short telling how he came to write the Holmes stories and how much he enjoyed hearing from Holmes's admirers in all parts of the world.

In 1931 Herbert Wilcox produced *The Speckled Band,* with Raymond Massey as Holmes. Once again the setting was modernised, complete with dictaphones, secretaries and sliding panels. To successfully divorce Holmes from the Victorian era in which he was originally conceived, the actor portraying him must be suitably Sherlockian. Unfortunately, despite his consummate acting ability, Massey failed to convince. Athole Stewart supported as Watson while the suitably malevolent Lyn Harding played Dr Rylott. The plot followed the Conan Doyle story, in which the villain, with the aid of a snake, tries to murder his stepdaughter so he can take over her inheritance. The director Jack Raymond does manage to produce some eerie moments in the old dark house, but all in all it remains an unremarkable film.

The year 1932 saw Gainsborough Pictures present yet another version of *The Hound of the Baskervilles* with Robert Rendel as Holmes and Fred Lloyd as Watson. Despite the good production qualities and excellent lighting and photography the film fails to do justice to Conan Doyle's tale and some of the onus for this must fall on Edgar Wallace who worked on the scenario and produced a confusingly vague and pedestrian screenplay. The film relies heavily on dialogue rather than sustained action or mood and there is a lack of any real excitement. Like many other versions of the tale it had quite an elaborate reconstruction of the Baskerville legend, presented this time as a prologue.

Despite a good attempt by Robert Rendel to present a fully convincing Holmes he fails somewhere along the line. His interpretation of the character is an intelligent well considered one suggesting intellectual certainty, but fails to convince as a contemplative deducer. His physical appearance does not measure up to the conception of Holmes: he was short of stature and lacked the angular features so typically Sherlockian. As one contemporary reviewer comments: 'Rendel acts well but he is not Holmes.'

If it appears that the majority of the Holmes interpreters of the early thirties were in general a little disappointing, there was however one man who more than satisfied – Arthur Wontner.

Arthur Wontner in his third Holmes feature *The Missing Rembrandt* **(1932).**
Twickenham Film Studios Ltd

Chapter 5

Critics' Choice

OF all the actors to peer out from under the brim of a deerstalker and exclaim 'Elementary, my dear Watson', none has received more acclaim from the film critics and Holmes purists than Arthur Wontner. Doyen of Sherlockian scholars, Vincent Starrett in *The Private Life of Sherlock Holmes* said of Wontner:

> . . . no better Sherlock Holmes than Arthur Wontner is likely to be seen and heard in pictures, in our time. Sentimentalised, as is imperative, his detective is the veritable fathomer of Baker Street in person. The keen worn, kindly face and quiet prescient smile are out of the very pages of the book.

Lady Jean Conan Doyle in a letter to Wontner expressed her delight in 'your really splendid acting . . . [and] masterly presentation of Sherlock Holmes.'

It is surprising then that this man, whom one film critic called 'the perfect Holmes', is virtually unknown today and rarely thought of in the context of the great detective. This cannot be due to his lack of output, for over a seven year period he starred in five Holmes features. The reason probably lies in the fact that, unlike the later screen exploits of Holmes, Wontner's films are never shown on television and as a result have virtually become lost to the general public, although the Sherlock Holmes Society of London does screen some of them from time to time.

So although Wontner is not a name that immediately springs to mind when the movie Holmes is being discussed, it would be remiss of me not to spend some time considering him and his portrayal of the master detective which made such an impact on the film critics.

Arthur Wontner was born in London in 1875 only twelve years before Holmes himself made his literary debut. Wontner was first and foremost a stage actor and it was in the theatre that he made his name. His biggest successes include *Ben Hur* (1912) and the original Baldassare in *The Maid of the Mountains*. He played Laertes to Henry Irving's *Hamlet* and Bassanio to Beerbohm Tree's Shylock in *The Merchant of Venice*. He had been in films off and on since 1915, but it was not until he starred as Holmes that he really caught the attention of the cinema audiences.

It was Twickenham Studios, an ambitious independent company, that brought Wontner's Holmes to the screen. The films, which lack the polish of the Hollywood features of the same period, place their stories in the present, and despite the fact that they clearly exhibit signs of their limited budget by relying heavily on interiors, they are competent and efficient efforts.

It was however the faithfulness of the characterisation of the great detective that was the real appeal of these films. As one critic put it: 'Wontner's characterisation of Sherlock Holmes is superb, both his facial resemblance and his bearing of quiet confidence supplying to the last degree the traditional Holmes.'

The first of Wontner's Holmes films was *The Sleeping Cardinal* released in July 1931. The story was a clever blending of two Conan Doyle stories: *The Empty House* and *The Final Problem*. It was the longest of the Wontner films, the slowest paced, but in many ways the best. Its leisurely pacing allowed Holmes ample opportunity to exhibit his remarkable powers of deduction. The deductions all arise out of the plot and are cleverly handled so that they never go beyond the bounds of plausibility. The film's director, Leslie Hiscott, never underestimates the intelligence of the audience with the sudden and illogical presentation of facts and deductions that the film does not substantiate.

Ian Fleming (no relation to the creator of James Bond) made a likeable but rather stupid Watson. One of the major faults with most Holmes films is the presentation of a Watson as a mere buffoon to emphasise Holmes's brilliance. After all the 'real' Watson was no idiot; without him there would be no Holmes saga to relate. Norman McKinnel appeared as Moriarty.

The film opens with an impressive bank raid, in which the night watchman is murdered and although the safe is broken into, nothing appears to have been touched. Holmes later discovers that in fact the genuine notes have been replaced with excellent forgeries.

Sherlock Holmes (Arthur Wontner, seated) looking very smug in a scene from *The Sleeping Cardinal* (1931). *Twickenham Film Studios Ltd*

Our attention is then turned to Ronald Adair, a young Foreign Office official, who has been cheating at cards. Under the threat of exposure by a criminal gang he is persuaded to carry counterfeit notes to the Continent under the cover of his Foreign Office passport which protects his luggage from examination.

Holmes, appealed to by Adair's sister to cure his gambling habits, senses a connection between her brother's dilemma and the mysterious bank robbery. Holmes is, of course, correct and it is not long before he is visited by the heavily disguised head of the international criminal gang who warns the detective to keep his nose out of their affairs. Holmes notices a peculiarity in the villain's upper molar and discloses to Watson later that the man is none other than their long-standing adversary, Moriarty.

Following up a clue of a boot-tag which he had noted on Moriarty's left boot, Holmes, with aid of Lestrade and a body of police, raids a mysterious boot-maker's cellar where a printing press is found. There then follows an attempt on Holmes's life by shooting at him from the building opposite his rooms. But the detective foils the attempt, and Moriarty is brought to justice.

The misleading title refers to an innocent-looking oil painting of the same name behind which Moriarty has a secret room. When the film opened in America it was called, more appropriately, *Sherlock Holmes's Fatal Hour*.

The Americans were very kind to the film placing it on the same plane as Hitchcock's *Blackmail*, which at that time was regarded as the best British talkie ever produced. As for Wontner, the American critics were unanimous: *The Bioscope* said that: 'the poise and intelligence of Mr Arthur Wontner's characterisation of Sherlock Holmes makes it the most distinguished yet on the screen, superior even to the interpretations of Clive Brook and John Barrymore'. Another critic remarked: 'Twickenham Studios has put the real Holmes on the screen and has created a picture which will please anyone who knows the character in its literary form'.

Wontner's second Holmes feature was *The Sign of Four* made in 1932. This film, in which Ian Hunter took over temporarily as Dr Watson, was directed by the British veteran, Graham Cutts. It relies heavily on the Conan Doyle novel and tends to lose most of its grip by presenting a prologue which gives the whole plot away, leaving the matter of detection too obvious to be of any great interest.

The Sign of Four was not as happily received as *The Sleeping Cardinal*; many reviewers criticised the photography and lighting. However Wontner himself was praised again for his Holmes interpretation – as the *Picturegoer* put it: 'Arthur Wontner is as usual, a perfect Holmes'.

Ian Fleming returned as Watson in *The Missing Rembrandt*, a satisfying mystery with a good cast, (including Miles Mander and Frances L. Sullivan), made in the latter part of 1932. Leslie Hiscott also returned to direct, and although the early part of the film is very slow in tempo, the atmosphere of Limehouse and Baker Street is realistic and all through there is an air of respect for the Holmes tradition.

The plot is loosely based on Conan Doyle's story *Charles Augustus Milverton*. Sherlock Holmes is asked by the French authorities to investigate the theft of a Rembrandt from the Louvre. The villain is introduced to us in a Chinese opium den. He is Baron von Guntermann, and it is not long before Holmes, leaving Scotland Yard well behind, is on his trail. Guntermann's accomplice, Carlo Ravelli, carrying out a blackmail threat, provides some valuable clues from which Holmes is able to establish Guntermann's guilt.

Holmes's deductions tend to be a little far fetched compared with the previous two films, and Wontner in this feature began to deviate slightly from his original conception of the character, portraying the detective with a marked air of facetiousness. Nevertheless, he was the best Holmes around at the time and he returned in 1935 with Fleming in *The Triumph of Sherlock Holmes*.

Sherlock Holmes (Arthur Wontner) and Watson (Ian Fleming) in their Baker Street chambers as seen in *The Missing Rembrandt* (1932). *Twickenham Film Studios Ltd*

This feature had the benefit of a superb Moriarty in Lyn Harding, who was virtually repeating the role he first played against Raymond Massey's Holmes in the 1931 production *The Speckled Band*. Harding gave size and strength to the role.

The Triumph of Sherlock Holmes was based on Conan Doyle's novel *The Valley of Fear* and sets a great deal of its action – energetically if not too convincingly – in America's West. Leslie Hiscott directed once again, and, although

Left: Sherlock Holmes (Arthur Wontner), in retirement, studies a book on bee-keeping in an early scene from *The Triumph of Sherlock Holmes* (1935). *Real Art Productions Ltd*

Below: Dr Watson (Ian Fleming), Sherlock Holmes (Arthur Wontner) and Inspector Lestrade (Charles Mortimer) prepare an ambush for Moriarty in *The Triumph of Sherlock Holmes* (1935). *Real Art Productions Ltd*

the plot stays fairly close to the book, it has an interesting variation at the beginning which shows Holmes actually in retirement looking after bees. The climax of the film involves a gun battle between Holmes and his arch enemy. While he is fleeing up the staircase of a ruined tower Moriarty is hit by a bullet from the detective's gun and falls, to what most certainly is his death.

However, Harding scored such a success as Moriarty that the character

Sherlock Holmes (Arthur Wontner) examines some evidence in *Silver Blaze* (1937).
Twickenham Film Productions Ltd

was resurrected for him to play again in Wontner's fifth and final Holmes feature, *Silver Blaze*. This film, directed by Thomas Bentley, again uses a Conan Doyle story as its basis and embellishes it with the presence of Moriarty. Here he is attempting to prevent a horse entering a big race, which seems rather small beer after his previous activities involving international criminal machinations.

Silver Blaze was, despite the consummate playing by the trio of leading actors, the weakest and dreariest of the series and on its release in Britain in 1937 it received such a cool reception that it was thought not worth releasing in the States. However it was finally shown in America in 1941 under the title of *Murder at the Baskervilles* which would seem like an obvious attempt to cash in on Twentieth Century Fox's 1939 success, *The Hound of the Baskervilles*.

All in all it was an enjoyable series, but compared with the later Holmes features, the films appear very dated, slow and cumbersome. But why, in spite of this, does not Arthur Wontner's highly praised portrayal of Holmes tower above the films to be remembered today? I feel the critics overstated the case in calling him 'the perfect Holmes', for, despite the consummate playing of this sensitive actor, he falls short of presenting the definitive Sherlock Holmes.

He was, by the end of the series, over sixty and he appeared far too frail to be the incarnation of the Holmes as represented in Paget's drawings. His delivery also, while assuring the audience of his intellectual prowess, was so casual and relaxed that he failed to capture the quixotic and capricious nature of the man. The whole interpretation, though in the right mood, lacked energy. There is a certain *je ne sais quoi* about Holmes which is difficult to define, but one is aware when an actor fails to capture this. For me Wontner failed to convince fully.

After the mid-thirties, interest in Holmes as a movie subject waned, but by the end of the decade the detective's fortune took a decided turn for the better when Hollywood came up with a new version of *The Hound of the Baskervilles* and a new dynamic Holmes.

Chapter 6

The Ideal Holmes

THE actor who has come nearest to creating the definitive Sherlock Holmes on screen is Basil Rathbone and it was he who donned the deerstalker for Twentieth Century Fox's version of *The Hound of the Baskervilles* in 1939.

Basil Rathbone was born in Johannesburg, South Africa in 1892. His father was a British mining engineer, and after some unpleasant encounters with local natives, he decided to send young Basil to England to be educated at Repton College. At the age of eighteen Rathbone went to work as an insurance agent but he really wanted to become an actor and in 1911 he managed to get a job with Sir Frank Benson's touring company. He made his stage debut at Ipswich playing Hortensio in *The Taming of the Shrew*. However, the First World War interrupted his career. He became a captain in the Liverpool-Scottish regiment and was awarded the MC.

Rathbone made his film début in 1921 in the British film *The Fruitful Vine*, but this was just a brief interlude between plays. In the mid-twenties he journeyed to America, where he settled and spent most of the rest of his life.

Although Rathbone did not lack work in silent films, it was not until the arrival of the talkies which utilised his beautiful, crisp speaking voice that he made his mark on the movie-going public.

During the next decade he appeared in supporting roles in some of the great films of the thirties: *Anna Karenina*, *David Copperfield*, *Captain Blood*,

Romeo and Juliet, The Adventures of Robin Hood, The Tower of London. In 1939 this polished performer was cast as the famous Baker Street detective – a casting which was to leave its mark on cinema history.

Rumour has it according to Michael B. Druxman's *Basil Rathbone, His Life and His Films* (New Jersey: Thomas Yoseloff Ltd, 1975) that it all started at a Hollywood party: Darryl Zanuck, Gregory Ratoff and writer Gene Marker were discussing new properties to screen when one said: 'Somebody should do these damned Sherlock Holmes stories.' Another asked: 'Whom would you get to play Sherlock Holmes?' 'Whom else, but Basil Rathbone.' None of the trio was quite sure who made the fateful utterance, but within months of the conversation Rathbone was introduced to both radio listeners and moviegoers as Sherlock Holmes.

The casting cannot be considered anything other than inspired. Rathbone presented an ideal picture of Holmes: he was tall, carrying himself with an erect guardsman-like bearing, with an extraordinary angular face, a long aquiline nose and a defiant jawline. His voice was sharp and incisive, yet dark with a majestic quality betraying his stage training. He portrayed Holmes as an alert, energetic, capricious and sardonic animal. Rathbone played with great style and authority; it was a part for which he obviously had a great deal of affection, and it showed.

The Rathbone Holmes found immediate acceptance with the public – though not always with critics – resulting in over two hundred broadcasts and more than a dozen films.

In 1939 the detective film which had fallen into a rut of the formularised 'B' pictures could hardly have had a more stylish and impressive showcase than Fox's *Hound of the Baskervilles*, the first Rathbone-Holmes vehicle which initiated the equally inspired casting of Nigel Bruce as Watson. Bruce's characterisation which bore little relation to the Watson of the Conan Doyle stories, was little more than the same silly ass Englishman he played in countless other films; but it was all the same an act of great charm and turned Watson into an endearingly avuncular figure.

Probably the best of the many versions of *The Hound* it remains an impressive handsomely mounted and certainly respectful treatment of the Conan Doyle novel, even if it is a little too measured in its pacing and never quite makes the most of its potential.

Ernest Pascal's literate script keeps quite close to the original novel and where innovations have been made, they are pertinent and effective. As for example the seance where Dr Mortimer's wife in a trance-like state attempts to contact the dead spirit of Sir Charles Baskerville. 'What happened that night on the moor, Sir Charles?' she asks. The only reply is the low eerie howl of a hound far out on the moors.

There is some fine dialogue too. When Watson, reunited with Holmes on the moor, asks what is going on, the detective replies:

Murder, my dear Watson. Refined, cold-blooded murder. There's no doubt about it in my mind, or perhaps I should say in my imagination, for that's where crimes are conceived and where they're solved – in the imagination.

Watson: But there's been no murder . . . unless you mean Sir Charles and the facts clearly indicated he died from heart failure.

Holmes: That's why so many murders remain unsolved, Watson. People will stick to facts, even though they prove nothing. Now if we go beyond facts and use our imagination as the criminal does, imagine what might have happened, act upon it as I've been trying to do in this case, we usually find ourselves justified.

Dr Mortimer is presented as a sinister figure with pebble glasses and a

Basil Rathbone in classic Sherlockian garb, with Nigel Bruce in *The Hound of the Baskervilles* (1939). **Compare this scene with the Sidney Paget illustration on page 14**
Twentieth Century Fox

black beard, giving Lionel Atwill a marvellous red-herring role, much favoured with low key close ups. The villain's wife in the novel becomes his sister, presumably in order to make her a more acceptable romantic partner for Sir Henry Baskerville, played by Richard Greene, who incidentally had star billing above Rathbone and Bruce.

Others in the impressive, practically all-English cast are John Carradine as the butler Barryman (sic) and Mary Gordon who played Mrs Hudson: a role she was to repeat in future years.

The hound itself is shown without any spectral phosphorus adornment and the emphasis is put on the fact that it is a real. ferocious dog: the result is genuinely frightening. The legend of the Baskervilles, told in flashback at the beginning of the movie, shows the hound attacking Sir Hugo Baskerville at the throat. The scene, set on the moor and shown in silhouette, is very effective.

The director, Sidney Lanfield, usually at home with light comedies, made fine use of shadows and the impressive gothic mist-enshrouded moor sets, which were enhanced by the barely perceptible use of gauzes over the lens.

The most surprising aspect of the movie is the lack of background music,

'Murder, my dear Watson. Refined, cold-blooded murder!' Rathbone and Bruce in a scene from *The Hound of the Baskervilles* (1939). *Twentieth Century Fox*

which would have greatly added to the atmosphere of such scenes as the one near the end of the film where Holmes is tracking down the murderer across the dark misty moor. The reason not to use suitable background music appears to be a mystery in itself.

Rathbone was never better as Holmes. He kept his interpretation under firm control and presented the detective as a cool calm reasoner, with definite bohemian traits. There was a total lack of the smugness which dogged Brook's and Wontner's work, and, later, his own. Even when he appeared in disguise, as an old pedlar, he kept the characterisation well within the bounds of reality.

Holmes's deductions are pertinent and have an air of credibility, and he does not resort to the needle for inspiration during the action. The first and last reference to it comes in the final line of the film, when leaving Baskerville Hall drawing-room for his chamber, after announcing himself fatigued by his exertion, Holmes calls back to his associate: 'Watson – the needle.' Dr Watson picks up his medicine case and follows him out of the picture.

The film was an immediate success. 'The Americans have done right by Conan Doyle' was one British critic's view, while the *Kinematograph Weekly* commented: 'It is a grand Sherlock Holmes.'

What seemed to please and impress most people was the authenticity of the film which seemed a pleasant change after Brook's and Wontner's modern Holmes. Graham Greene in the *Spectator* wrote:

Dr Watson (Nigel Bruce) and Sir Henry Baskerville (Richard Greene) on the moor in *The Hound of the Baskervilles* (1939). *Twentieth Century Fox*

> In this new film Holmes is undoubtedly Holmes, and he hasn't to compete desperately with telephones and high speed cars and 1939. 'Your hat and boots, Watson, quick. Not a moment to lose!' He rushed into his room in his dressing gown and was back in a few seconds in a frock coat. The atmosphere of unmechanical Edwardian [sic] flurry is well caught: the villain bowls recklessly along Baker Street in a hansom and our hero discusses plans for action in a four wheeler.

It is amusing to relate how the *Motion Picture Herald* saw the film's selling points: 'The obvious exploitation cue is for a strong campaign addressed to the millions who have read the book, and such other millions who have not got round to reading it, but have meant to for some time, and now under the circumstances needn't.'

For whatever motive the millions had for going to see *The Hound of the Baskervilles,* see it they did and made it one of the most successful films released in the first half of 1939.

The film was also a triumph for Basil Rathbone: 'he is the ideal selection for Holmes' commented one critic, and although not all critics were convinced of this, the public were unanimous in applauding the Rathbone interpretation.

Because of the film's success, Fox hurried a sequel into production: *The Adventures of Sherlock Holmes.* This time Rathbone and Bruce got the top billing they deserved. The new production was officially based on the Gillette play, but the final product bears little resemblance to it, or to the two other previous films which had supposedly used the play as their source. Screenplay writers Edwin Blum and William Drake added much new material and rejected a lot including, happily, Holmes's romantic entanglement. The main similarity between this film and the play was the high-pitched battle of wits between Holmes and Professor Moriarty.

The plot with its complicated convolutions deals with Moriarty's attempt to commit the 'most incredible crime of the century': the theft of the crown jewels. He attempts to blind Holmes to his machinations by providing a bizarre problem to occupy his mind. 'I am depending on it to absorb Mr Holmes's interest, while I am engaged elsewhere. I'll give him a toy to delight his heart, so full of bizarre complications that he'll become completely involved', Moriarty tells one of his underlings.

The 'toy' is revealed to Holmes when he is visited in his Baker Street rooms by Ann Brandon (Ida Lupino) who is almost on the verge of hysterics. Her brother Lloyd has received a grotesque note – the drawing of a man with a strange bird hanging round his neck – exactly like a warning note which preceded her father's brutal death ten years earlier. Holmes immediately tackles the problem, and while he sends Watson off to spy on Miss Brandon's suspicious fiancé, he visits the Kensington museum where he determines the strange bird to be an albatross. 'This is no childish prank, Miss Brandon, but a cryptic warning of avenging death. We must go to your brother at once' cries Holmes. But unfortunately he is too late. Lloyd Brandon is found murdered in the street. Holmes deduces the weapon used is a weird one, which first strangles and then crushes the skull.

From then on Holmes becomes deeply involved with the Brandon affair, as Moriarty hoped and neglects a threat to the safety of a precious stone the 'Star of Delhi' as a trivial matter. As a result Watson deputises for Holmes when the diamond is transported to the Tower of London for safe keeping, while the detective, in one of his most successful disguises as a music-hall entertainer, attends a garden party where he believes an attempt will be made on Ann Brandon's life. He is correct. Hearing her cries from a nearby park, Holmes rushes to the spot just as a dim figure is about to hurl a Patagonian bolas, a weapon consisting of three long strands of rawhide each tipped with leather coated lead balls. Holmes knocks Ann to the ground and the bolas winds itself around a statue, snapping off the head.

Holmes shoots at the fleeing assailant and wounds him. He is captured and admits he is one Gabriel Mateo whose father was murdered by Ann's

Bruce, Rathbone and Ida Lupino as Anne Brandon in *The Adventures of Sherlock Holmes* (1939). *Twentieth Century Fox*

father who had stolen his South American mine. Mateo reveals that it is Moriarty who has urged him to seek revenge. Holmes then realises that Moriarty has used these crimes to shield a greater one.

In something of an anti-climax, the detective hurries to the Tower of London where he is just in time to prevent Moriarty stealing the crown jewels. After a struggle on the top of the Tower, a blow from Holmes causes the master criminal to fall to what we must presume to be his death.

Despite the screenplay's shortcomings (how, for example, Moriarty knew the exact ancient Inca funeral dirge Ann Brandon had heard before her father's death is never explained; nor is it clear how he came to know of the cryptic significance of the albatross), the film maintains the high standard that *The Hound of the Baskervilles* had set, and in many respects it is a better film. Alfred Werker was a fine director and he set the action at an exciting pace, while making full use of Fox's impressive London sets, creating an authentic period atmosphere. We are treated to some superior vignettes, such as the thrilling scene involving the killer garbed in a South American gaucho outfit, with close ups of his grotesque club foot moving slowly and deliberately in pursuit of the heroine through the fog-shrouded park at night.

In general the film was well received although many reviewers thought there were too many loose ends for complete credulity. One perceptive American critic did make the observation that even the English climate seldom has thick fogs in May.

Moriarty was played with all the supercilious truculence the part requires, by George Zucco, a British actor who made a career of playing villains in Hollywood features of the thirties and forties. (In fact he was to pit his wits against Rathbone's Holmes on a later occasion.) Zucco made Moriarty a suave and smug character who obviously enjoyed evil for evil's sake. The ultimate purpose behind his machinations was to beat Sherlock Holmes. As Moriarty replies to one of his minion's remarks 'Holmes again?': 'Always Holmes – until the end.'

When the two antagonists appear together on screen (which is all too infrequent) the dialogue fairly bristles. As when, for instance, near the beginning of the film, just after Moriarty has been found innocent of a murder charge owing to lack of evidence, he and Holmes meet outside the court.

Moriarty: I am afraid you have a bad opinion of me, Holmes.

Holmes: On the contrary, I hold you in the highest esteem, but only as a knave.

Moriarty: May I give you a lift. Cabs are scarce in this rain.

Holmes: Thank you.

Moriarty: After you, my dear Holmes.

Holmes: By no means, I prefer that you precede me at all times.

Moriarty: What a creature of habit you are.

Holmes: You've a magnificent brain, Moriarty. I admire it. I admire it so much I'd like to present it, pickled in alcohol to the London Medical Society.

Moriarty: It would make an impressive exhibit.

The rest of the dialogue does not quite come up to this level, but never the less there is an air of Holmesian authenticity about it. As, for example, when the detective discusses the murder of Ann's brother: 'Brandon was strangled to death', Holmes declares, 'the wounds on the back of the head were administered post mortem, which introduces an interesting element. They were unnecessary therefore vicious. Intelligent criminals are seldom vicious, and though the apparent method of the crime was brutal, I am convinced the crime itself was intelligently planned.' Conan Doyle himself would surely not have been ashamed of that exposition.

Nigel Bruce's Watson was, as before, no fit companion, one might think, for the intellectually brilliant Holmes, but a likeable buffoon of a man.

Rathbone was again, excellent; his timing and phrasing seemed to echo the Holmes of Conan Doyle's pages, while he cuts a figure reminiscent of the Paget drawings. Rathbone was never again to achieve this peak of performance, later a certain tiredness with the character made him exaggerate Holmes's idiosyncracies to the detriment of his portrayal. Also, sadly, it was the last time Rathbone was to play the detective in period. He was never again to stride through the fog in his Inverness cape and deerstalker. But, as regards the quantity of films, Rathbone's career as Sherlock Holmes had hardly begun.

Chapter 7

The Baker Street Dozen

THE quality of the two Fox films was such that under ordinary circumstances a series would have been a forgone conclusion. But by the end of 1939 the Second World War had broken out and foreign agents and spies were much more typical and topical than the antiquated criminal activities of Moriarty and his like. Probably Fox saw the Holmes series as too dubious a commercial proposition for continuance on the same level of high budget production and too difficult to relegate to their 'B' picture series. So Fox dropped Sherlock Holmes, although Rathbone and Bruce did continue to play their roles on radio.

In February 1942 Universal pictures acquired the screen rights of Sherlock Holmes from the Conan Doyle estate and immediately put Rathbone and Bruce under contract for a proposed series of Holmes films. Thus one studio was continuing a series originated by another, using the same leading actors.

At Universal Holmes was presented as a contemporary figure, allowing him to be placed into stories involving the then topical World War. The updating also eliminated any budget problems concerning period sets and costumes which had been lavish in the Fox films.

There was an outcry at first against this modern Holmes from the purists even though Universal explained the change with an opening title about Conan Doyle's character being timeless. In all fairness it is unlikely that the series would have pleased Holmes's creator, but although the settings were modern, exchanging the hansom cab for the motor car, and most of the plots bore little relation to the original stories, the playing and much of the writing were in character.

Some of the Holmes 'props' remained – the pipe and violin for instance, but the famous fore and aft deerstalker was dispensed with. In the first film of the series Holmes is about to don this anachronistic headgear when Watson rebukes him with, 'Holmes, you promised.' 'Oh, very well,' replies the master detective, putting on a fedora instead.

Nigel Bruce carried on with his bumbling portrayal of Watson, appearing to better effect without the dyed hair and moustache he had in the Fox films. Mary Gordon appeared again as Mrs Hudson; she never did very much, but she was always there. One remembers her comforting remark to Watson in *Spider Woman* when the good doctor believes Holmes is dead: 'Now, sir, cheer up; what cannot be cured must be endured.'

The Universal series has received some harsh words from the critics and film historians, who have accused the films of being shoddy productions with Rathbone hamming the role of Holmes. It is true to say that the films are far from being works of art, but this is something they never set out to be. Their

Basil Rathbone sporting his special Sherlockian hairstyle in *Sherlock Holmes in Washington* (1943). *Universal*

aim was simply to be entertaining 'B' pictures and certainly this modest ambition was realised. As to Rathbone's acting, certainly he treated the role flamboyantly and as the series wore on he did tend to overact as a reaction to the boredom of playing the same character, but after all Holmes was a very singular and flamboyant character. In fact in the first film in the series one character refers to the detective as being 'unorthodox and theatrical'. The series, despite its many shortcomings, was highly enjoyable, and had a fine panache which many 'B' thrillers of the same period lacked.

Sherlock Holmes and the Voice of Terror was the initial offering with Holmes being asked by Sir Evan Barham (Reginald Denny) of the Inner Council, the government's secret defence committee, for help in putting an end to Nazi saboteurs operating in Britain, as well as uncovering the person or persons behind a series of frightening radio broadcasts in which acts of aggression such as train crashes and warehouse fires, are foretold by one who identifies himself only as the 'Voice of Terror'.

On Holmes's first visit to the Council's chambers, he exhibits his skill of deduction by observing that one of the council members, Admiral French, objects strongly to his being called in. When asked how he could possibly infer this, Holmes replies: 'From the carpet: a man who rises from his chair and digs his heels sternly into the carpet is violently opposed to something, and the Admiral, being quite distressed by the criticism of the press concerning the Council's handling of the Voice of Terror would be most apt to resent my intrusion.'

Later when a knifed corpse is dumped on his doorstep, Holmes gets a further opportunity to exercise his deductory powers by pointing out to Watson that the knife was thrown by the tip from a distance of about fifty feet by a man about five foot ten. 'How can you know that?' asks the incredulous Watson. 'Elementary,' comes the reply, 'no fingerprints.' As for the distance and the man's height: 'the angle of entry and the force with which it penetrated the victim'.

The corpse leads Holmes and Watson into the 'dark and sinister alleys of Limehouse', and eventually to a bombed hill-top church. It is within this large structure that Holmes foils the Nazi invasion bid and reveals that the Voice of Terror is none other than the head of the Inner Council – Sir Evan Barham. Holmes then gives an incredible explanation of how a member of the British peerage came to be a Nazi spy:

> You see, Sir Evan Barham is not Sir Evan Barham. In March 1918 Lieutenant Evan Barham was a prisoner in a German prisoner of war camp. There, his amazing resemblance to a certain Heinrich von Bork, a brilliant young member of the German secret service, sealed young Barham's fate. One morning he was taken out and shot; murdered in cold blood. Barham had no immediate family. The details of his private life were avidly studied by

von Bork who was three years at Oxford and had a perfect knowledge of the English language and English habits. So, with possibly the help of a little plastic surgery, not forgetting the considerable resemblance to Barham in the first place, the deception was carried through.

When asked what made him first suspect Barham was an imposter Holmes replies succinctly: 'The real Sir Evan carried a scar from childhood – this one is only twenty years old: a detail, but significant'.

The film ends with Holmes and Watson standing in the bombed church watching the dawn coming up over the English Channel with Holmes reciting a patriotic little homily; a device which was to become a feature in most of the films.

The dialogue in this instance was lifted straight from Conan Doyle's *His Last Bow:*

Watson: It's a lovely morning, Holmes.

Holmes: There's an East wind coming, Watson.

Watson: I don't think so. Looks like another warm day.

Holmes: Good old Watson. The one fixed point in a changing age. But there's an East wind coming all the same. Such a wind as never blew on England yet. It will be cold and bitter, Watson, and a good many of us may wither before its blast. But it's God's own wind none the less. And a greener, better, stronger land will be in the sunshine when the storm is cleared.

Beautifully read, with Rathbone's voice getting full strength out of the flow of words, it's a moment which never fails to stir. Here is the quintessence of Holmes and Watson. Optimistic Watson, easy-going, bluntly honest and devotedly loyal. Eccentric Holmes, capricious, full of unexpected humours and odd enthusiasms, neurotic – but with a powerful sense of right and wrong. Friends, despite the opposite paths of their personalities, for ever.

And so the first rather pleasing entry in the Universal series ends. Some footage depicting control switches being moved to effect a train wreck was lifted from Universal's *The Invisible Man*, 1933, and the impressive bombed church set was used two years later for *The Mummy's Curse.*

The second film in the series, made the same year, *Sherlock Holmes and the Secret Weapon,* utilised Holmes's propensity for using disguises by presenting Rathbone as a Swiss inventor, a criminal Lascar and an old German bookseller, ('I have some works of an old German writer – Wilheim Shakespeare').

The plot involved the Nazis again and Holmes's attempts to stop them getting their hands on the 'secret weapon'. This is a new bomb-site invented by a Swiss scientist, Professor Tobel, who is kidnapped by 'one of the most brilliant men in the history of crime', Holmes's old arch-enemy Professor

Moriarty, now in league with the Nazis. The only indication as to the whereabouts of the bomb-site is the clever cipher left behind by the inventor. The cipher, borrowed from Conan Doyle's story *The Dancing Men,* is eventually cracked by Holmes and it leads him inevitably to Moriarty's lair. The macabre climax finds Holmes playing for time by submitting to an operation whereby Moriarty attempts to systematically drain all the blood from his body.

'You were a stimulating influence to me, Holmes, but it was obvious I should win in the end. Each second a few more drops leave your desiccated body. You can feel them can't you? You're perfectly conscious aren't you?' gloats the arch-criminal. But, apparently undaunted, Holmes, understandably looking pale and wan, replies with his old conceit: 'I shall be conscious long after you're dead, Moriarty!'

This utterance proves to be prophetic because after the inevitable timely interruption by Watson and the police, Holmes, with outstanding energy for a man in his condition, gives vigorous chase to the escaping Moriarty, arranging for him to plunge to his doom through a 'highly deceptive trap-door' into the sewers below, whence he would rise again later in the series.

Moriarty was played with great relish by the ubiquitous Universal heavy, Lionel Atwill, who had previously confronted Rathbone's Holmes as Dr Mortimer in *The Hound of the Baskervilles.* It is in *Sherlock Holmes and the Secret Weapon* that Moriarty, believing the great detective to be dead, utters the memorable line: 'Brilliant man Sherlock Holmes, too bad he was honest.'

This film introduces Inspector Lestrade of Scotland Yard, a thick-skulled, but likeable policeman who became a regular in the series appearing in six of the films, and who, with Watson, provided most of the comic relief.

The closing patriotic speech mis-quotes *Richard II*: Watson: This little island is still on the map. Holmes: Yes, this fortress built by Nature for herself, this blessed plot, this earth, this realm, this England.

Towards the end of 1942 the third film of the series was completed: *Sherlock Holmes in Washington.* The story was penned by Bertram Millhauser who was a one-time director of silent serials and was the scenarist of the 1932 Fox film, *Sherlock Holmes.*

The film opens revealing Holmes in sparkling form as he expresses surprise at Watson's decision not to go to Lords cricket ground that afternoon. Typically, Watson, not having voiced his intention, is amazed that Holmes can know this, and asks him how he does. 'Elementary, my dear Watson,' comes the inevitable reply, 'invariably when you go to a cricket match you fill your flask with my best whisky. Just now I noted in passing that the flask was empty. A single whiff informed me that it had recently been filled. Obviously after filling it you had poured the contents back into the bottle. Therefore, you had changed your mind about the cricket match.'

The plot centres on some secret documents which the detective is told by a Home Office official are 'of such great international importance, that if they fell into the hands of the enemy it would be absolutely disastrous for Britain and her allies'. Both the documents and the agent who was carrying them have disappeared in America. On the instigation of the British Government Holmes takes up the case and, after preliminary investigations, he comes to the conclusion that the agent destroyed the original documents after microfilming them and concealing the microfilm in an American match folder.

Washington is the next stop, but not before the enemy 'the most insidious international spy ring that ever existed', make an attempt on the lives of Holmes and Watson, by dropping a large piece of masonry from the top of a building. Luckily Holmes is alert to the danger and the stone misses them.

The search for the microfilm constitutes the rest of the film, and cameraman Lester White, who had filmed the previous two adventures, had to continually concentrate on the match folder as it passed from one person to another, each unaware of its secret. After some rather preposterous deductions, Holmes's investigations lead him to a bogus antique shop in Washington where the villain has his headquarters.

Posing as an eccentric collector, Holmes enters the shop and manages to come face to face with the head villain. George Zucco, who gave such a fine portrayal as Moriarty in *The Adventures of Sherlock Holmes*, 1939, again confronted the detective, this time as Richard Stanley, the evil head of the spy ring. He sees through Holmes's disguise and there then follows a scene which contains some splendid icy, urbane barbs between the two men, each an expert in his field, either side of the law. Holmes ironically suggests to Stanley that the documents he seeks might have been reduced in size for easy transportation while Stanley lights a cigarette using a match from the very match folder which conceals the microfilm. 'The man who has the documents doesn't know it,' says Holmes with a wry grin.

As it often did, Holmes's omniscient nature reached almost unbelievable but amusing heights when, placing an urn before a large antique chest, he walks round it and then calmly throws up the lid, triggering a spear which smashes the urn and Stanley's hope for a dead Sherlock.

The climax is a little disappointing, although the closing moments do feature the usual stirring speech. Holmes and Watson are being driven past the famous buildings of Washington when Holmes remarks:

> This is a great country, Watson. Look up there, ahead – the Capitol: the very heart of this democracy. It's not given to us to peer into the mysteries of the future, but in the days to come, the British and American people will, for their own safety and good of all, walk together in majesty, justice and in peace.'
>
> 'That's magnificent, I quite agree with you,' says Watson.
>
> 'Not with me,' answers Holmes, 'with Mr Winston Churchill. I was quoting from a speech he made not so very long ago in that very building.'

The triumphant music swells and heralds: 'The End'.

In the first three films Rathbone's hair was arranged, or disarranged, in a peculiarly dishevelled manner which was rather unnecessary. There appears to have been no reason for this unless it was to endow Holmes with an 'arty' bohemian look. However this affected style was dispensed with in the first film made in 1943, the fourth in the series: *Sherlock Holmes Faces Death.* In this film Rathbone appeared with his hair brushed straight back emphasising his finely chiselled, intellectual features.

Sherlock Holmes Faces Death was a departure from the war theme which had been predominant in the earlier films, and concentrated more on the mystery elements in the story which included a sprinkling of references to the supernatural, howling winds, secret passages and reports of a homicidal ghost:

Watson: Ghosts don't stab people in the neck do they? Or do they?
Holmes: Not well bred ghosts, Watson.

The film opens on an eerie note, with shrieking winds, a clock striking thirteen and an attempted murder. All this takes place at Musgrave Manor in Northumberland; an old country house turned into a home for convalescent officers. Watson, who is in charge of the home, decides, as soon as the 'dark deeds' begin, to call on Sherlock Holmes for help. He arrives at Baker Street early one morning. 'What brings you from Northumberland at such an early hour?' inquires the dressing-gowned detective as they tuck into one of Mrs Hudson's breakfasts. 'A bad business, Holmes, a very bad business; but how do you know I come from Northumberland?' Holmes smiles at Watson's puzzlement, 'Elementary, my dear Watson, your over-night bag carries a fresh custom label: the only train to arrive at Euston Station at this hour is the Northumberland Express from Newcastle. Ergo, Sir Knight, thou comest from Northumberland.' And so with the aid of a thorough knowledge of his *Bradshaw*, Holmes completes another smart piece of deduction.

It is not long before the famous pair set off for Musgrave Manor, which is peopled with the strangest suspects, some of whom are highly disturbed officers suffering from various forms of battle fatigue. They arrive in time to greet Inspector Lestrade and find the first in a series of corpses.

The highly ingenious plot manages to involve a thread from one of Conan Doyle's stories, *The Musgrave Ritual,* and one of the most memorable scenes in the film is where the Musgrave family are gathered to hear the reading of the ritual by Sally Musgrave (Hilary Brooke): the custom being that after the death of a Musgrave, the next in line should recite the ritual in the presence of the rest of the family. In the middle of the narrative a clap of thunder fills the gigantic room and a bolt of lightning crashes through a window toppling a suit of armour.

The ritual is apparently meaningless:

Where was the light on the face of the messenger?
Where did he speed?
To guard the queen's page.
Who to repell?
The King's cautious page.
What then this disaster?
Page slaughters page.
Who came to slay him?
The bloodthirsty bishop.
Where shall he go?
Deep down below.
Away from the thunder,
let him dig under.

But Holmes manages to make sense of it: 'This is no gibberish: Kings, bishop, page – these are chess terms and there,' exclaims Holmes, pointing at the chequered floor of the grand hall, 'that's the chess board. The secret of the Musgrave murders is locked up in that floor, and, by jove, we've got it.' By using the floor as a giant chess board and real people as the pieces Holmes manages to discover the Musgrave treasure which turns out to be an ancient land grant.

Basil Rathbone and Arthur Margetson in *Sherlock Holmes Faces Death* (1943). *Universal*

In order for the murderer to reveal his identity and to elicit a confession from him, Holmes places himself in a vulnerable position and allows the villain to trap him in the subterranean crypt of Musgrave Manor. As he tells Watson: 'These egomaniacs are so much more chatty, when they feel they have the upper hand'. Although the murderer (Arthur Margetson) manages to grab Holmes's revolver from him, the detective never really faces death, for the gun contains blank cartridges: 'A cheap sort of trick, I grant you, but I had to have the confession.'

The homily at the end is one of the most stirring. As Holmes and Watson are riding through the countryside in an open car on their way back to Baker Street, the detective is provoked into philosophical thought:

> There's a new spirit abroad in the land. The old days of grab and greed are on the way out: we're beginning to think what we owe the other fellow, not what we're compelled to give him. The time's coming, Watson, when we shan't be able to kneel and thank God for blessings before our shining altars, while men anywhere are kneeling under physical or spiritual subjection. And, God willing, we'll live to see that day.

In the dark days of the war, emotions must have run high on hearing this potently patriotic speech, beautifully delivered by Rathbone.

The village used in *Sherlock Holmes Faces Death* was originally constructed on the Universal lot for the Frankenstein productions of the thirties, but was utilised by a number of their other productions of the thirties and forties.

Rathbone and Bruce next appeared as the famous pair in a guest star scene in the 1943 Olsen and Johnson comedy, *Crazy House*. The film opens as word reaches Universal Studios in Hollywood that the comedy team of Olsen and Johnson are coming. Andy Devine rides down a western street with his rasping voice echoing: 'Olsen and Johnson are coming.' Leo Carrillo clears another western set telling his amigos the same news. The scene cuts to Basil Rathbone dressed as Sherlock Holmes. Nigel Bruce as Watson, comes to tell him the important information, but Holmes is already aware of the fact. 'I know, Watson, Olsen and Johnson are coming.' When asked how he knows, Rathbone replies: 'I am Sherlock Holmes, I know everything.' Although this scene was meant to be a light-hearted skit on the Holmes character, it does tend to reflect the flaw in many of the Universal Holmes films: Holmes's omniscience. He is never wrong and in some cases he is aware of facts which he could have gleaned only by committing the crimes himself or by having a close relationship with the screenplay writer. A few chinks in Holmes's armour would have brought more credibility to the plots.

The next Holmes film proper dropped the Sherlock Holmes prefix and was called *Spider Woman*. The film was given this rather macabre and garish title, it would seem, in an attempt to attract the horror devotees as well as the

Holmes aficionados. Although Bertram Millhauser skilfully blended elements from Conan Doyle's *The Sign of Four* and *The Dying Detective* into his own screenplay, the adventure turned out to be one of the lesser instalments in the Holmes Universal casebook.

At the beginning of *Spider Woman* Holmes fakes his own death, fooling even Dr Watson, so that he can set a trap for the criminals behind a series of deaths known in the press as 'pyjama suicides', so called because: 'each and everyone of them went quietly to bed and rose up in the night and killed himself'. Holmes tells Watson and Lestrade that he believes these suicides to be murders: 'brilliantly conceived and executed, they are near to being perfect crimes'. For no sound reason, other than the methods involved in the suicide/murders being 'peculiarly subtle and cruel, feline not canine', the master detective believes that the gang behind the crimes is headed by a woman: 'a female Moriarty'.

Holmes notes that all the victims are 'fairly well-to-do and fond of the gaming table'; he considers this latter fact the only real clue and, acting on it, he enters the gambling world disguised as a distinguished native officer, Rahjni Singh. In this disguise it is not long before he comes in contact with the 'female Moriarty' herself, Andrea Spedding, played by Gale Sondergaard, an excellent villain. Holmes discovers that she selects her victims from those desperately in need of money, persuades them to pawn their life insurance with her various accomplices and then kills them. He becomes a willing victim in order to detect the method of the murders, which he does after narrowly missing death himself. Holmes discovers that small spiders are introduced into the bedrooms of the suicide victims: '*Lycosa Carnivora*, its venom once injected into the bloodstream causes such excruciating agony that the victim is driven to self-destruction.'

But the case is far from complete: the detective is still in the dark as to how the spiders get into the locked rooms: 'We know only half the machinery of these crimes'. But one clue does come to light after the unsuccessful spider attack on Holmes: near the outer entrance of the ventilator he finds the footprint of a child.

The master's next move is to visit Matthew Audway, the man who may have supplied Andrea Spedding with the deadly spiders, for as yet Holmes has 'not one shred of evidence to connect this woman with her crimes'. On interviewing the man calling himself Audway he becomes convinced that he is an imposter. Holmes explains:

> You called these glass cases, cages; any scientist would call them terrariums. You said the poison of the *Lycosa Carnivora* was valuable to doctors; any

The Spider Woman (Gale Sondergaard) plots another diabolical murder with her henchman Norman (Vernon Downing) in *Spider Woman* (1944). *Universal*

> scientist would say the virus was valuable to toxicologists. You said you were told the Black Widows eat their mates; any scientist would know it. Just now you said you could get me a *Mendex Flagrante – mendex flagrante* is Latin for flagrant liar. Obviously you are not Matthew Audway.

The imposter makes a dash for it, upsetting some of the terrariums and as a result Holmes and Watson are unable to give chase. After dealing with the escaping spiders, they find the dead body of the real Audway and a copy of his diary which records his travels in the jungles of South Africa. They find a reference, in abbreviated form, to something or someone who is immune to the virus of the *Lycosa Carnivora.* This is baffling until Watson, stumbling into a cupboard, finds the chart of a skeleton. 'I thought Audway's interest was invertebrates not vertebrates. Why the chart of the skeleton of a child?'

'It isn't a child,' corrects Watson, 'look at these teeth. The skull of a normal child of this size would be much larger in proportion to the circumference of the chest.'

'I've got it,' snaps Holmes, 'the perfect instrument for the Spider Murders – able to creep through the smallest openings. Watson, if you ever see me getting cocksure again, fancying myself more clever than Andrea Spedding, just whisper to me – pygmy!'

And so Holmes sets off for the fairground, 'For of all places we may find a pygmy, a sideshow is most likely.' It is in the fairground that the Spider Woman finally gets her clutches on the detective, providing the film with an exciting finale. Holmes is tied behind a metal caricature of Adolf Hitler in a shooting gallery, his heart being in direct line with the bull's-eye, while Watson and Lestrade, quite oblivious of this, fire live ammunition at the target. Of course they never quite hit the bull's-eye and Holmes does manage to escape. Later when Watson asks him if he was playing any of the games he replies: 'Yes, but my heart wasn't in it.'

Inevitably the Spider Woman and her gang are rounded up, including the pygmy and taken away by Lestrade and his men. The closing sequence, minus a homily this time, is interestingly dramatic with more than a touch of Alfred Hitchcock. Holmes remarks that the centre of a throng of people is the ideal place for a murder:

> In an isolated place a cry for help or a single shot might well arouse the curiosity of at least one casual witness, but in an arcade, like this, people are bent only on pleasure and will instinctively disregard any deviation from the normal that doesn't immediately involve them. Yes, it's the most logical spot in the world to commit my murder . . . in the middle of a crowd!

As Holmes is saying this, both he and Watson are gradually lost by the camera, and are swallowed up by the carnival crowd.

Although Holmes never tackled the Spider Woman again, she did return to the screen in a film of her own, *Spider Woman Strikes Back* (1946).

'There's blood on the moon tonight', said the poster advertising the next Holmes film, *The Scarlet Claw*: probably the best of the Rathbone series. The opening sequences rank highly among macabre movies: the fog drenched marsh, cut to the old church, a close-up of the tolling bell within, then a far shot of the small town followed by the interior of a tavern and the silent, frightened faces therein as each wonders why the bell is tolling at such a late hour. The scene is La Mort Rouge (the red death) a small village in Canada, a place far more foreboding than anything that England had to offer ('More's the pity, Watson').

Holmes and the good doctor are in Quebec attending a convention on the occult when they receive a telegram from Lady Penrose of La Mort Rouge, expressing a fear for her own life, and begging Holmes for help. Minutes later they hear of Lady Penrose's grim death. Her body has been found in the church of the village – with her throat torn out. 'Consider, Watson, the irony, the tragic irony: we've accepted a commission from the victim to find her murderer. This is the first time we've been retained by a corpse!'

When the famous pair arrive at La Mort Rouge they find hostility among the villagers, including the murdered woman's husband, Lord Penrose (Paul Cavanagh), who believes his wife's death has been caused by the legendary monster of La Mort Rouge, which has recently reappeared on the marshes around the village. Drake (Ian Wolfe), Penrose's butler, comments: 'I saw it last night, moving in and out of the shadows.' The 'it' is later seen by Dr Watson who aptly describes it as 'a ball of fire-spitting flames'. Holmes, of course, is convinced that this monster is no *ignis-fatuus*, but a clever criminal who has recreated the monster as a screen for a series of gruesome murders.

Holmes's first clue arrives when he sees the corpse of Lady Penrose and recognises her as a one-time actress, Lilian Gentry. The detective then goes in search of the monster on the treacherous fog-bound marshes. His investigations convince him that 'our antagonist is not a phantom'. When Watson enquires how the monster could manage the flames, Holmes replies: 'Merely clothing treated with phosphorus. When the murderer fled his shirt caught on a tree and this piece of cloth was torn off.'

The piece of cloth begins a trail which leads to the murderer whom Holmes realises is an actor, Alistair Ramson, who murdered a fellow actor in a jealous rage over Lilian Gentry. Ramson was believed to have been killed while escaping from prison two years previously. Holmes still has the problem of identifying the actor who is a master of disguise: 'Alistair Ramson has established a character, perhaps several others, who are by now familiar to the people of La Mort Rouge and quite above suspicion.'

Holmes discovers that two other inhabitants in the village had connections with the Ramson case. One of them is Judge Brisson (Miles Mander), the magistrate, now retired, who passed sentence on the actor. But the detective is unable to save Brisson's life for Ramson, disguised as Nora the housekeeper, murders the judge.

Holmes cleverly discovers Ramson's hideout and is confronted there by the mad actor armed and disguised as a fisherman. Holmes asks him quite coolly why he murdered Lady Penrose:

> 'I see no reason why I shouldn't tell you. I couldn't bear the thought of another man possessing her.'

Nigel Bruce and Basil Rathbone confront Arthur Hohl in *The Scarlet Claw* (1944). *Universal*

'And Judge Brisson?'

'During the trial I grew to hate him and when he sentenced me to prison, I vowed someday I would escape and kill him.'

'Obviously you plan still another murder, otherwise you would have returned to the safety of your first disguise, and defied me to find you.'

'You're right, I am! There were three people in my life who had no right to live. Two have already died. The third remains. Tonight I will kill him.'

Before Holmes can learn the identity of the third person, Watson blunders into the room, falling down the stairs and switching the lights out. In the confusion that follows, Ramson escapes. Holmes nevertheless thanks Watson for his intrusion, and then fills the doctor in about the facts:

'This Ramson is a paranoic, and his orgy of crime is not yet completed.'

'Where d'you think he'll strike again?'

'Obviously Journet is to be his next victim. As in the cases of Lady Penrose and Judge Brisson, Journet also felt Ramson's presence, but in each case it was vague and unexplainable. Journet was a guard at Tallon Prison where Alistair Ramson was confined. He is the third person against whom the murderer holds a grievance.' Watson then informs Holmes that Journet, the hotel keeper, has disappeared. 'Journet's disappearance can mean only one thing: he's in hiding. Our job is to find him before Ramson does. Journet is the only man who can lead us to the murderer.'

But another murder comes before Holmes finally apprehends the villain. Journet's daughter, Marie (Kay Harding), in refusing to reveal her father's whereabouts to Ramson, signs her own death warrant. Her death assures Holmes even more that Ramson's present disguise is that of a person accepted without suspicion by the whole village.

Eventually Holmes finds Journet (Arthur Hohl) and after telling the news of his daughter's death, enlists his help in setting a trap for the killer. Watson spreads the news that he and Holmes are giving up the case and going back to England immediately. Journet makes a point of letting everyone know he is going to the church across the marsh to offer up a prayer to Marie. Out in the marshes Journet is attacked by Ramson in his disguise of Potts the postman, only to find he is really attacking Sherlock Holmes – who has exchanged places with Journet. 'You realise you'll never hand me over to the police alive,' cries Ramson as he dashes off into the mist into the arms of the vengeful Journet who kills him with his own weapon, a four-pronged garden weeder – the scarlet claw. 'Ramson's instrument of death has been his own executioner' comments Holmes.

The homily which concludes the film, spoken by Holmes in the car on the way to the airport, is a good one:

'Canada, the lynch pin of the English-speaking world whose relations of friendly intimacy with the United States on the one hand and her unswerving fidelity to the British Commonwealth and the Motherland on the other. Canada: the link that joins together these great branches of the human family.'

'Churchill say that?'

'Yes, Watson, Churchill.'

After *The Scarlet Claw* any film in the Holmes series would seem to be an anti-climax. *The Pearl of Death* was doubly so for it presented one of the weakest villains of the series: Giles Conover (Miles Mander, who played Judge Brisson in the previous film and who appeared in Wontner's 1933 Holmes film *The Adventures of the Missing Rembrandt*) who was a pale creature by the side of Moriarty or Ramson. However, Holmes apparently had high regard for him, as he told Watson:

> This man pervades Europe like a plague, yet no one has heard of him. That's what puts him on the pinnacle in the records of crime. In his whole diabolical career the police have never been able to pin anything on him. Yet give me crime without motive, robbery without clue, murder without trace, and I'll show you Giles Conover.

The screenplay by Bertram Millhauser is a new working of Conan Doyle's *The Adventure of the Six Napoleons* and centres round the theft of the Borgia pearl: 'The blood of twenty men on it down through the centuries'.

Immediately following the theft from the Royal Regent Museum, Conover is apprehended and searched but the pearl is not found. Holmes, certain of Conover's guilt, is baffled. Ironically the detective's first break comes when he hears of another crime: the murder of a retired colonel. It is not so much the crime as the method that interests Holmes. The victim's back was broken – a method used by a grotesque killer known as the Hoxton Creeper: 'A monster, Watson, with the chest of a buffalo and the arms of a gorilla. His particular method of murder is back-breaking and it is always the same – the third lumbar vertebra – the Hoxton Creeper has always been Giles Conover's right arm when it comes to killing.'

The body is found in a pile of broken china, plaster ornaments and bric-a-brac. Holmes tells the bewildered Lestrade: 'That's the outstanding feature of this case. Why was all this china smashed and nothing else disturbed? Why?'

Holmes is certain there is a connexion between this murder and the theft of the Borgia pearl: 'My surmise is that Giles Conover has lost the Borgia pearl, and is trying desperately to get it back just as we are.'

There then follow two attempts to murder Holmes. One involves a book which, when opened, shoots a dagger out, but Holmes is too cautious to be

The poster advertising *The Pearl of Death* (1944). *Universal*

caught out by this and the dagger ends up in the ceiling of his Baker Street chambers. He expresses his gratification at these murder attempts; Watson, as usual, is amazed. 'Conover wouldn't go to all this trouble to eliminate me if I weren't in his way because he hasn't found the Borgia pearl', explains the detective.

It is not long before Lestrade informs Holmes of another murder – 'a little old lady with her back broken, and found in a litter of smashed china'. On reaching the scene of this second murder, Holmes suggests to Lestrade

Sherlock Holmes and Sgt Thompson (David Clyde) examine the murder weapon in *The Scarlet Claw* (1944). *Universal*

that the china was smashed deliberately after the murder was committed and not as a result of a struggle. 'If you lift up that body I think you'll find there's not a vestige of broken china underneath.'

A third identical murder follows the second. Holmes begins to examine the smashed china. 'Why smash the china?' asks Watson.

'The killer didn't choose to smash the china, he had to. Possibly to cover up something else that was smashed. Some object identical in all three cases, the clue that we're looking for.'

Holmes eventually determines that the object that links the murders is a small bust of Napoleon. 'Why smash Napoleon?' asks the doctor. 'Think, Watson, think! Something was hidden in one of those busts, something that Conover was searching for – the Borgia pearl!'

Holmes discovers that Conover, on the day of the theft of the pearl from the Royal Regent Museum, was able to place the pearl in one of six wet plaster busts of Napoleon before being apprehended. Holmes then follows up the trail of the remaining busts and the climax comes when, in disguise, he substitutes for a would-be victim and awaits the arrival of Conover and the Creeper.

However, the Creeper overpowers the detective and he appears to be at the mercy of the two villains, but by cleverly talking to the Creeper and convincing him that Conover means to doublecross him, Holmes manages to grab a gun while the brute killer attacks Conover.

Holmes smashes the final Napoleon bust and reveals the Borgia pearl – 'with the blood of five more victims on it'.

'Well, at least Conover was one of them,' assures Watson.

'What's Conover? No more than a symbol of the greed and cruelty and lust for power that have set men at each other's throats down the centuries. The struggle will go on, Watson, for a pearl, a kingdom, perhaps even world dominion, until the greed and cruelty are burned out of every last one of us. When that time comes, perhaps even the pearl will be washed clean again.'

The Creeper was played by Rondo Hatton, a grotesque-looking actor who suffered from acromegaly, a disease which distorts and enlarges the facial features. The director, Roy William Neill, made the most of Hatton, usually filming him in scenes with deep shadows and low key lighting. Hatton, who was known as the only horror star to play monsters without make-up, played the Creeper again in several non-Holmes films, including *The House of Horror* (1945) and *The Creeper* (1946).

The House of Fear, which bears no relationship to a feature of the same title released by Universal in 1939, was completed by December 1944, but was not released until well into 1945. The screenplay inspired by Conan Doyle's story *The Five Orange Pips* was written by Roy Chanslor and provided Holmes with one of his most baffling mysteries.

The films opens with Holmes being visited by a Mr Chalmers, the underwriter of an insurance firm:

'The events I am about to relate began a fortnight ago, in a grim old house perched high on a cliff on the west coast of Scotland. This singular structure is known as Drearcliffe House. Gathered there were the seven members of a most extraordinary club called "The Good Comrades". Into this unique gathering came their melancholy housekeeper, Mrs Monteith, bearing a message for Ralph King, a retired barrister. King received it casually. When they saw the contents of the envelope, the Good Comrades took the whole thing as a joke, but their housekeeper was right: it was no laughing matter. For on the following night, Ralph King died horribly, his body being mutilated. This was only the beginning. A few nights later, as the Good Comrades

Rathbone and Bruce in a posed shot from *The Pearl of Death* **(1944).** *Universal*

gathered to drink a final toast to their departed member, Mrs Monteith came in with another envelope, this time addressed to Stanley Rayburn, in his day a distinguished actor. This time you may be sure there was no laughter. These men were afraid and their fear was justified. Once again the message proved to be a portent of death. It was ten days before Rayburn's battered body was recovered.'

'Tell me, Mr Chalmers, what did these envelopes contain?' asks Holmes.

'In the first case, seven orange pips; in the second case, six!'

'A moment ago you referred to this club as extraordinary. Why?'

'All the members are past middle age, retired and without near kin. Six months ago they formed this club here in London and promptly left for Drearcliffe, the ancestral home of a Mr Bruce Alistair, their eldest member.'

'Nothing very remarkable about that,' comments Watson. 'Sounds rather friendly.'

'Shortly after forming this club,' continues Chalmers, 'all these seven men changed their insurance policies making the other members their beneficiaries. The policies total over £100,000. What worries me, Mr Holmes, is . . .'

'. . . whether these two deaths were accidental or not,' interrupts Holmes.

'Exactly. Of course, I may be wrong, I have no proof, but it's just possible that one of these men plans to murder the others one by one.'

'And collect on all the policies. I see the whole thing,' beams the doctor.

'Bravo, Watson! But why the orange pips?'

Watson is unable to answer this puzzling query and this aspect of the affair so intrigues Holmes that he decides to tackle the case.

When Holmes and Watson arrive at Drearcliffe (where, as legend has it, no man goes whole to his grave) there is another corpse: Guy Davies, 'burnt to a crisp' in the furnace – 'we identified him by his cuff links'. Davies was also the recipient of orange pips: five this time.

Holmes decides to call in Scotland Yard and Inspector Lestrade arrives in due course, and while he and Watson go around making wild theories as to the motive of the crimes, Holmes studies the behaviour of the remaining Good Comrades, each of whom acts in the manner of a true red herring.

Three more deaths occur, each leaving the body unrecognisable. Mr Bruce Alistair (Aubrey Mather) being the only remaining member of the Good Comrades, Lestrade jumps to the obvious conclusion: 'He killed 'em all, one after another, for the insurance money.' Holmes denies this and reveals to Lestrade a sliding panel which leads to a secret passage down below to the old smugglers' den at the base of the cliff. There he and Lestrade discover the six Good Comrades alive and well. As Holmes explains:

Mr Alistair's completely innocent. They selected him as their dupe. Whenever

> there was a funeral in the neighbourhood they dug up the body and dressed it in the clothes of their members. Then they staged a fake death and mutilated the body beyond all recognition. In the meantime the so-called 'corpse' disappeared quietly into the smugglers' room underneath Drearcliffe House.

And so ends one of the neatest and most effective of the Universal Holmes mysteries. Throughout, the special effects department was kept busy with providing howling winds, thunder and lightning which, added to the dimly lit interiors, give the film a suitably mysterious and sinister mood.

The Woman in Green followed in 1945 and saw the re-emergence of Moriarty, this time played at his best by Henry Daniell. Bertram Millhauser returned to provide what was to be his final screenplay which contained elements from Conan Doyle's *The Adventure of the Empty House* and Gillette's play.

The plot involved Holmes and Watson with what the press called 'The Finger Murders' – 'the greatest crime wave since Jack the Ripper'. Attractive women are being murdered and found minus a right forefinger. Holmes theorises:

> 'Watson, I am convinced that these murders are only incidental to some larger and more diabolical scheme. I rather think that they're not the work of any one man.'
>
> 'Come now, Holmes, you don't expect me to believe that there's a whole organisation going and killing people and chopping off their fingers.'
>
> 'It's possible. Quite possible.'
>
> 'Well, whoever is behind all this must be out of his mind.'
>
> 'On the contrary, my dear fellow, if my assumptions are correct, this little scheme has behind it the most brilliant and ruthless intellect the world has ever known.'
>
> 'You don't mean Professor Moriarty?'

Holmes does, and it is not long before the evil genius visits the detective to warn him off. This scene contains the famous interchange which is to be found in *The Final Problem* and Gillette's play:

> Moriarty: Everything I have to say has already crossed your mind.
>
> Holmes: And my answer has, no doubt, crossed yours.

The murders prove to be an ingenious vehicle for blackmail. Rich victims are chosen and persuaded that they have committed one of the 'Finger Murders'. Holmes is baffled as to the method used in persuading the victims they have committed 'these atrocious murders'. But after an attempt on his life is made by a sniper who, Holmes discovers, is in a trance, he has the answer.

He explains to the baffled Watson:

Hypnotism! A diabolically simple technique. The severed finger is what links the blackmail victim to the murder. He wakes, finds the grisly thing in his pocket and doesn't know how it got there. He has no idea he has been hypnotised, for all he knows he may have committed the atrocious crime during some dreadful lapse in sanity. At the state that he is utterly demoralised, the blackmailer steps in. They swear they saw him commit the murder, and, being human, the victim will pay anything rather than stand trial on a charge which will make his very name loathsome.

The sniper, while still in a trance, mentions a woman, and on this slender clue Holmes goes to the Mesmer Club, where he meets the lovely hypnotist, Lydia (Hillary Brooke) who is in fact in league with Moriarty.

Lydia invites Holmes back to her flat for a nightcap, and there she puts him under hypnosis. Moriarty then arrives on the scene, believing he has at last got the detective in his power. To check that Holmes is not faking the hypnotic trance, Moriarty cuts his hand with a knife; Holmes does not flinch. The master criminal then leads him to a parapet, but before Moriarty is able

Sherlock Holmes and Inspector Lestrade (Dennis Hoey) round up the rascally members of the Good Comrades in *The House of Fear* (1945). *Universal*

to instruct Holmes to jump, Watson and the police arrive.

Holmes then reveals that he was not in the least hypnotised but was in fact: 'holding the fort until the arrival of the law. I substituted a drug of my own for the one this dear lady pressed on me. A drug that, although it leaves the subject conscious, renders him quite insensitive to pain. That accounted for my lack of reaction to the knife.'

Moriarty, seeing the game is up, attempts to jump to the building opposite, but fails and lands in the street below. This time, as far as Rathbone's Holmes was concerned, it was the end of the 'Napoleon of crime'.

Holmes looks out over London and reflects: 'The stars keep watch in the heavens, and in our own little way we too, old friend, are privileged to watch over our city'.

Pursuit to Algiers showed a decided decline in inventiveness and proved to be the weakest of the series. The screenplay was written by Leonard Lee and bore a faint resemblance to Paramount's *The Return of Sherlock Holmes* in that most of the action takes place on board an ocean liner.

Holmes and Watson are engaged to escort Prince Nikolas, the heir to an Eastern throne, to Algiers. Once on board ship Nikolas is passed off as Watson's nephew but this does not seem to fool a group of assassins also on board who wish to kill the prince in order to seize political power in their country.

The plot which gives Holmes little opportunity for making many deductions is heavily padded with the inclusion of two musical numbers and some amusing but unnecessary comedy scenes with Watson.

One of the dramatic highlights of the film occurs when one of the villains Mirko (Martin Kosleck) throws a knife through an open porthole into what is apparently the inert body of the prince. However, Holmes, alert to this danger, has substituted a dummy in the bed and is waiting on the other side of the porthole to slam it down on the killer's wrist. 'How unfortunate Mr Mirko. These porthole covers are notoriously treacherous, I am afraid you've broken your wrist. You shouldn't have played shuffleboard today, you know. When I saw that skilful hand and that unerringly accurate eye of yours, I remembered the Circus Medlara in Paris and your amazing exhibition of knife throwing. Goodnight!'

The detective's counter-measures thwart the villains, until, towards the movie's conclusion, it seems that the antagonists have won out by kidnapping the prince. But, of course, this is not so, for it is revealed by Holmes that the young man posing as Nikolas is not really the heir, but a decoy. The real Nikolas turns out to be a steward whom the enemy could have successfully snatched at any time. A neat conclusion to what was, on the whole, a rather dull episode in Rathbone's Holmes career.

Martin Lowry, who played John Stapleton, the murderer in *The Hound of the Baskervilles* (1939), is seen aboard the ship as a passenger named Sanford.

In 1946, *Terror by Night*, the penultimate movie in the Universal Holmes series, and incidentally the shortest, was released. Frank Gruber, who wrote the original screenplay, provided a tightly plotted story, which, save for the brief opening sequences, takes place entirely on a train speeding through the darkness from London to Edinburgh.

As the train leaves Kings Cross Station, Holmes explains to Watson that the reason for their journey is to see that Lady Margaret Carstairs' famous diamond, the 'Star of Rhodesia', gets safely back to its vault in Edinburgh. Watson suggests that it is a routine police job, but Holmes disagrees: 'That's where you're wrong, old fellow. An attempt to make away with it in London was unsuccessful. A second attempt, in all probability, will be made on this train.'

Once the express gets under way so does the plot. The camera darts from the cab of the train, to exterior shots, then down the corridor and into a compartment just as Lady Margaret's son (Geoffrey Steel) falls to the floor, dead.

With the trip barely begun it would seem that Holmes has failed already, having not only a theft to deal with but a murder as well. Inspector Lestrade,

Inspector Gregson (Mathew Boulton) and Holmes (Basil Rathbone) attempt to question the hypnotised sniper (Tom Bryson) while Watson (Nigel Bruce), as usual, looks on. A scene from *The Woman in Green* (1945). *Universal*

who is also on the train, is not convinced that a murder has been committed. But, says Holmes:

> Consider the facts, Lestrade. Young Carstairs was dead when the jewel was taken, otherwise he would have put up a struggle, and there were no marks of violence on the body. If, however, he died a natural death, we must assume that the thief just happened to be on hand just at the right moment, which is outside the realm of probability. No, Lestrade, in this case nothing was left to chance – that's why I say, find the murderer and you'll find the diamond.

Holmes, while doing some investigation on his own in the luggage van, is kicked out of the train by the unseen killer. The detective, desperately clinging to the side of the fast-moving train, manages to edge his way down the side of the carriage to a door and re-enter the train, shaken but unharmed. Holmes is now certain that the luggage van contains a vital clue to the whole mystery. He returns with Watson and Lestrade and examines a coffin which is being transported to Scotland. He discovers a secret compartment, below the main section of the coffin:

> 'There's where your murderer has been hiding, Lestrade.'
>
> 'Then it's just a question of finding him, Mr Holmes,' replies the cocky policeman.
>
> 'Not him – them. This affair is obviously the work of two men: the one who planned it and the one who hid in the coffin and at a pre-arranged time emerged to commit the murder and effect the robbery.'

It is at this point that Holmes reveals that in fact the Star of Rhodesia has not been stolen. As with the young king in *Pursuit to Algiers*, the master detective had employed the use of a decoy, and he has the precious original which he hands over to Lestrade.

Holmes then discovers the guard who has been murdered by 'an air pistol which fires poison darts made of a gelatine preparation that melts in the wound'.

The villain is revealed as Major Duncan Bleek, professed friend of Dr Watson, but who in reality is Colonel Sebastian Moran, a henchman of the late Professor Moriarty. After Moran's accomplice, Sands (Skelton Knaggs), the dwarf-like murderer, secures the real diamond by knocking Lestrade unconscious, he himself is murdered by Moran.

However, Holmes is on to Moran, and when, as a precautionary measure, the Colonel has arranged for some of his men disguised as the police to board the train in Scotland to take him into 'custody', Holmes plunges the carriage into darkness and effects a quick change of captives. The pseudo Scottish officials end up with Lestrade, while Holmes retains the Star of Rhodesia and Moran.

Moran was played by Alan Mowbray who played Inspector Lestrade in the World Wide Production, *A Study in Scarlet.* Silent comedian Billy Bevan, also in that 1933 movie, played a train attendant.

Not only is *Terror by Night* one of the most effective of the Holmes series, but it is one of the most original murder-on-the-train movies ever made.

The final Rathbone Holmes film was released in the summer of 1946. It was known as *Dressed to Kill* in the States, but in Britain it was released under the title of *Sherlock Holmes and the Secret Code.*

We first discover Holmes railing Watson with some fine pseudo-Doyle dialogue, over the interpretation of his cases in the *Strand Magazine:* 'If you must record my exploits, I do wish you would put less emphasis on the melodramatic and more on the intellectual issues involved.' The story in question is *A Scandal in Bohemia* which features Irene Adler, whom, Doyle tells us, 'To Sherlock Holmes is always "the" woman'.

Mary Forbes, Billy Bevan, Alan Mowbray, Rathbone, Bruce and Dennis Hoey in a scene from *Terror by Night* (1946). *Universal*

'I do hope you gave "the" woman a soul,' says Rathbone scornfully as he tosses aside the issue of the *Strand Magazine*.

The plot, an original by Leonard Lee, begins when one of Watson's friends, Julian Emery (Edmond Brear), an ardent musical box collector, is attacked and burgled. Holmes is surprised to learn that only one inexpensive box has been stolen. He visits the collection of musical boxes and Emery shows him an almost identical box to the one which has been stolen. Holmes is intrigued by its unusual melody.

Shortly after this Emery is murdered and the musical box is stolen.

'That's the second attempt on this musical box – and this time it was successful.'

'But the box is only worth two pounds.'

'It was worth a man's life, Watson.'

Holmes's next move is to visit the auction rooms where Emery purchased the musical box. It is here he discovers that it was one of a set of three. The detective sets out to track down the other two. He finds the second, like the first, has been stolen, but is able to rescue the third before the adversaries get their hands on it.

It is at this point that Holmes learns that all three musical boxes were made in Dartmoor prison by Davidson, a criminal responsible for the theft of a complete duplicate set of Bank of England plates for printing five pound notes. As the plates have never been recovered, Holmes deduces that the secret of their hiding place is contained in the three musical boxes. With only one box in his possession, he has the problem of solving the riddle of all three.

'Somehow the tune is the key to the mystery. The variations in the way Emery's musical box played the tune are different from the variations in the one we have. You see, I took the trouble to memorise the tune that night we were with Emery in his flat.'

'Holmes, you amaze me.'

'Elementary, my dear fellow, one of the first principles in solving crime is never to disregard anything, no matter how trivial. Well, all we have to do now is to find the secret of the variations.'

It is Watson who eventually leads Holmes to the solution.

'I don't know one tune from the other. When I was a kid my people tried to have me taught the piano. I've always felt sorry for that old teacher of mine. Poor old girl finally reached the point of numbering the keys for me.'

'Numbering the keys, Watson!' exclaims Holmes. 'The nineteenth key of the keyboard is the nineteenth letter of the alphabet. You've solved it.'

The sleuth is now able to decode two thirds of the message: 'Behind books, third shelf, secretary, Doctor S . . .'

At this stage it is stalemate, with both Holmes and his antagonists needing one third of the message. However, the leader of the villains, Hilda Courtenay (Patricia Morison), a clever *femme fatale* stamped in the Irene Adler mould, manages to lure Holmes into a trap. He is left to die by suffocation from the exhaust fumes of a car, but he does manage to loose his bonds and escape.

In the meantime, Hilda Courtenay has fooled Dr Watson into revealing the whereabouts of the third musical box, with the use of a smoke bomb, much in the same way as Holmes used one in the Conan Doyle story, *Scandal in Bohemia.*

But all is not lost, for when Watson, attempting to look on the bright side, quotes Samuel Johnson, Holmes suddenly realises that he is the Dr S referred to in the secret message. Holmes and a body of police descend on the home of the famous doctor, now a museum, where they apprehend the villains who have just retrieved the precious bank plates from an old book secretary.

As the police take Hilda Courtenay away Holmes remarks to Watson: 'A brilliant antagonist. It is a pity her talents were mis-directed.' From this comment it would seem that 'the' woman now has a rival.

Chapter 8

His Last Bow

AND so *Dressed to Kill* became the final entry in the Universal series of Holmes films. In some ways it was ironic that it should now come to a close, for, after such a long period of opposition from the critics, the Holmes films were beginning to be accepted. Of this final film the British *Monthly Film Bulletin* said: 'Basil Rathbone continues his efficient characterisation of Holmes with good effect', while the *Motion Picture Herald* commented: 'it is exciting and suspenseful'.

However, further films were not to be. Posing in his Sherlock Holmes attire for a full page colour advertisement for Liggett and Myers Tobacco Company in a 1946 magazine in which *Dressed to Kill* was plugged, Basil Rathbone made his final bow as the Universal version of the ever famous detective. When the time came to renew his contract for more Holmes movies Rathbone had made the important decision: not to continue the series. 'I played Holmes for seven years, and nobody thought I could do anything else,' he explained. 'When I would come onto the set it was never "Hello Rathbone" – it was always "Hello Holmes".'

In addition to his film chores Rathbone, along with Nigel Bruce as Watson, played Holmes on radio. Asked by an interviewer the most difficult tongue-twister he had ever encountered in a script, Rathbone replied that in a Holmes radio show he was to have said: 'Watson, the board of directors is nothing but a horde of bores'. 'That', he added, 'was not how it came out.'

And so the film series ended; on the whole it had been an enjoyable one. A considerable part was played in its success by Roy William Neill, who directed eleven of the twelve films and produced nine. Neill, like Rathbone, became completely involved in the films and for the earlier episodes he brought in Thomas McKnight, a technical expert on Conan Doyle. He also worked on the screenplay of *The Scarlet Claw* and it is this film which typifies the talent of the man. His imaginative techniques are much in evidence throughout: Lord Penrose standing solemnly before the coffin of his murdered wife in a darkened room, photographed through a candelabra of lighted candles; the killer in the apparel of Nora the maid moving stealthily through the shadows towards the unsuspecting wheel-chair victim; the camera moving in for a close-up of a caged bird, chirping cheerfully, the only living thing to have seen the murder of the lovely teenaged girl.

After completing *Dressed to Kill* Roy William Neill stayed on at Universal and with Roy Chanslor (who wrote *The House of Fear*) and Saul A. Goodkind (film editor of the last three Holmes films) worked on *The Black Angel* with Peter Lorre. It was his last film, he died shortly after its completion.

The Holmes series had its own little repertory company of actors who appeared in different films in various roles. Apart from such regulars as Mary Gordon and Dennis Hoey there were Gerald Hamer (*Sherlock Holmes Faces Death, The Scarlet Claw, Pursuit to Algiers, Terror by Night*); Henry Daniell (*Sherlock Holmes and the Voice of Terror, Sherlock Holmes In Washington, The Woman in Green*); Hilary Brooke (*Sherlock Holmes and the Voice of Terror, Sherlock Holmes Faces Death, The Woman in Green*); Holmes Herbert (*Sherlock Holmes and the Secret Weapon, Sherlock Holmes in Washington, The Pearl of Death*); Paul Cavanagh (*The Scarlet Claw, The House of Fear, The Woman in Green*); Harold De Becker (*Sherlock Holmes and the Secret Weapon, Sherlock Holmes Faces Death, The Pearl of Death, The Woman in Green*); Miles Mander (*The Scarlet Claw, The Pearl of Death*).

Although Rathbone turned his back on Holmes in 1946, he was destined never to lose the Sherlock tag. After *Dressed to Kill,* he abandoned movies for a few years to do stage work which he found more rewarding and more refreshing in its change of pace. In 1953, however, at the age of 61 he donned the deerstalker once again. He opened at the Century Theatre on Broadway in the play *Sherlock Holmes.* It was a version of the Gillette play written by Ouida, Rathbone's wife. It was his first performance as the detective in seven years. Nigel Bruce had suffered a heart attack and was unavailable for the Watson role; Jack Raine played the good doctor. Unfortunately the show closed after three performances.

In a radio interview in 1958 Rathbone said of Holmes:

> I don't think the stories have lived because they were the best mystery stories, I don't think they are. What makes the stories live are the wonderful

characterisations Sir Arthur invented. Holmes is a much more important man than just a detective. He is a very remarkable human being. Watson was one of the most lovable characters of all time, and Moriarty was the most shrewd and vicious villain ever written. Doyle made them real people.

Rathbone confessed that after years of playing Holmes he began to dislike the man:

I once said to my wife the thing I would dread more than anything is to find myself seated by him at a dinner party because he'd frighten the day-lights out of me. I think playing him has given me a kind of inferiority complex. I was disturbed that people might think I was like that at home.

Whatever his feelings for Holmes he was never able to shake off the shadow of the great detective. In the late fifties as well as appearing sporadically in movies (*We're No Angels, The Last Hurrah, The Court Jester*) he spent a great deal of his time making records of the great classics, among these were some of Conan Doyle's Sherlock Holmes stories. A date with destiny was at last brought about: the true marriage of Conan Doyle's Holmes and Basil Rathbone. And yet these recordings are flawed to some extent by the fact that in telling the stories for the most part Rathbone has to assume the role of Watson, the storyteller, and not that of Holmes.

On 20 July 1967 Basil Rathbone was given a check-up by his physician, who found no signs of trouble. The next day he died of a heart attack. The actor who will be forever Sherlock Holmes in the minds of millions of movie-goers (and those who caught up with the detective's exploits on television), the ideal Holmes, had made his last bow.

Previous page: Sherlock Holmes, watched closely by Dr Watson, questions Mrs Monteith (Sally Shepherd), the housekeeper, about the mysterious orange pips in *The House of Fear* (1945). *Universal*

Sundry Sherlocks

AFTER the Universal series ended in 1946 it was not until 1958 that Sherlock Holmes made a major return to the screen, but in the meantime several small time Holmeses appeared on the scene.

In 1951 BBC television, successfully gathering momentum after the war-time shut-down, produced a series of six thirty-minute adventures based on the Conan Doyle stories. Alan Wheatley starred as Holmes.

Also in 1951 John Longdon appeared as Holmes in a cinema short, *The Man with the Twisted Lip*, based on the Conan Doyle story. The critics were unanimous regarding its quality, or rather lack of it. One critic stated: 'This three-reeler is directed and acted in a most shoddy manner and the plot development moves at some points at the most startling speed'.

Holmes is shown in the film to have a taste for brandy as well as tobacco, and Watson is breezily sketched by Campbell Singer. This film was probably meant to be the first of a series – but it sunk without a trace.

In 1954 a Franco-American television series of Holmes stories was produced by Shelden Reynolds in Paris. The series was never seen in Britain although the cast was entirely British. Ronald Howard (son of Leslie) was the detective; he was too young and too relaxed to be totally convincing, but nevertheless he made an interesting Holmes. Watson was played in the Nigel Bruce mould by Howard Marion Crawford, and Archie Duncan appeared as Lestrade in several episodes.

The stories, although presented in period, were original and bore titles such as *The Case of the Haunted Gainsborough* and *The Case of the Christmas Pudding*. The plots tended to be too whimsical and coy to have an authentic ring to them. Here is the synopsis of one such story, *The Case of the Unlucky Gambler*. A young boy comes to Baker Street to ask the great detective to find Herbert Fenwick, his missing father. Holmes agrees to tackle the case:

> 'Well Watson, we'll find that boy's father if we have to search every gambling den in England.'
>
> 'Gambling den?'
>
> 'Yes, didn't you notice the boy's clothing. The shoes were most expensive, but the coat was threadbare. The trousers come from the best haberdashery and the cap was ancient, attesting to the father's streaks of good luck and bad luck. There were other indications his father was a gambler. Young Andrew's speech, if you may recall, was sprinkled with the peculiar jargon of the gambler. Such terms as "touted off", "I'll give you odds" and "welching on a debt", the boy obviously learned from his father.'

Holmes learns that Fenwick owes money to several unworthy characters in the gaming underworld and deduces that his disappearance is a result of his inability to pay his debts. Holmes's trail leads him to an inn where he learns from the barman that Fenwick has committed suicide: 'He went down to the Thames and threw himself in. Left a note saying he couldn't go on.'

'Have they found his body?' asks Holmes.

'Oh not yet. Only his hat floating on the water.'

Holmes points out to Watson that this suicide was obviously faked to 'avoid his muscular creditors'. The detective suspects that Fenwick now plans to leave the country and is desperate enough to commit a robbery to get money to enable him to do so. However, Holmes manages to stop Fenwick from committing a robbery and persuades him to return home and face up to his debts. He then informs his young client that his father's disappearance is due to his undercover work for the government. Fenwick returns to the open arms of his son with the cry of, 'I'll never leave my family again'. And so the story ends with Holmes and Watson disappearing into the foggy night leaving a selection of loose ends untied.

Apart from these sundry Sherlocks, all was quiet on the Holmes front in the early fifties and so by 1958 the stage seemed set for the arrival of a new colourful version of 'Sherlock Holmes's most terrifying adventure'.

Holmes (Peter Cushing) questions Mrs Barrymore (Helen Goss) while Barrymore (John Le Mesurier) and Watson (André Morell) look on in *The Hound of the Baskervilles* **(1959).** *Hammer Film Productions Ltd*

André Morell and Peter Cushing in *The Hound of the Baskervilles* (1959).
Hammer Film Productions Ltd

Chapter 10

Hammer's Hound

IN 1954 a small British film company made a science fiction horror film which was perhaps the most important milestone in its history. Hammer Film's production of *The Quatermass Experiment* broke box office records in Britain. The film, a modest black and white effort, was based on a BBC television serial which had kept millions glued to their sets on Saturday nights. The success of this film led to an equally successful sequel which bore the uninspired title of *Quatermass II*.

Hammer chief, James Carreras, in an attempt to ascertain why these films had been so successful, ordered a questionnaire to be sent to every cinema manager who had shown the films. The results showed that the horrific aspects of the films were the real crowd pullers. When Carreras saw the figures, he decided to give the public a classic, 'a real good juicy Gothic thriller', to see what would happen.

Hammer took a calculated risk in resurrecting in technicolour Baron Frankenstein and his monster who had been last seen in the arid wastes of Abbott and Costello land. The risk paid off, for not only did *The Curse of Frankenstein* establish a new cycle of gothic horror films but it put Hammer films firmly on the international movie making map.

It is now difficult to appreciate the shattering effect that this new technicolour film *The Curse of Frankenstein* had on moviegoers at the time. By modern standards the film is very tame, yet at the time one critic suggested it should be given a new certificate SO: 'For Sadists Only'. Whatever the critics thought of the film did not stop it becoming a blockbuster on both sides of the Atlantic. The film also raised Peter Cushing who played Baron Frankenstein and Christopher Lee who played the monster to the level of international stardom.

The Curse of Frankenstein indicated the path to box office success and Hammer followed it with a remake of *Dracula* (*Horror of Dracula*, US title) again with Cushing who this time played Professor Van Helsing the scholarly Vampire expert, and Christopher Lee who played the Count. Not only was this a more competent film incorporating some superb moments of gothic terror but it was an even greater box office success.

The climax of *Dracula* has now become a classic: the Count trapped by Van Helsing in a shaft of bright sunlight crumbles magnificently into a small pile of dust which is scattered by the early morning breeze. There have been many variations on this theme but this still remains Dracula's most effective destruction.

With *The Curse of Frankenstein* and *Dracula*, Hammer seemed to have found the formula to success and they began to remake other classic chillers including *The Mummy*, *The Curse of the Werewolf*, *The Phantom of the Opera* and others. And so it was that in 1959 they came to dust off the old Conan Doyle novel *The Hound of the Baskervilles* to give it the Hammer treatment.

Hammer's production of the *Hound* was a technicolour version which concentrated on the grislier aspects of Conan Doyle's tale, in keeping with their previous horror successes.

Peter Bryan's screenplay uses the framework of Conan Doyle's story on which to hang some new and generally worthwhile innovations. The great problem facing any writer with the task of transferring this story to the screen is that Holmes is absent from the action for at least half of the book, reappearing as it were to tie up the loose ends. This may be acceptable for a book but not for a film whose selling power to some extent depends on the name above the credits. The actor playing Holmes must be well featured throughout the film to justify his billing. Peter Bryan managed quite skilfully to keep a fine balance between cinematic requirements and loyalty to the book.

The film opens with a reconstruction of the legend of the Baskervilles, in which the rascally Sir Hugo (David Oxley), pursuing a serving maid into some abbey ruins on Dartmoor, meets the hound of the Baskervilles – 'the hound from hell'. The scene fades to reveal that Dr Mortimer (Frances De Wolff) has been recounting the legend to Sherlock Holmes and Dr Watson in their Baker Street sitting-room. For aficionados of Holmes this room is a treat, for it is an almost perfect reconstruction of the room as recorded in Conan Doyle's stories, even to the small but important details of the Persian slipper filled with tobacco and a collection of bills transfixed to the mantelpiece with a knife.

'And what, may I ask, do you think of that, Mr Holmes?' asks Mortimer, referring to the legend. Holmes opens his eyes, gives a short exclamation and moves a chesspiece on the board at his side. He then addresses Dr Mortimer: 'There must be hundreds of similar folk stories I fail to see why I should find this one of singular interest.' This, the first sentence that the detective utters, sets the tenor for the whole interpretation of the character as set out by the script. The accent is on the capricious, arrogant, almost pompous facet of Holmes's nature. One reviewer called him 'waspish'. He takes no time out, like Holmes in the 'thirty-nine version, to crack a joke with Watson. He is at all times, as perhaps he should be, deadly serious.

But his arrogance is not without purpose. As in this instance, he later explains to Watson: 'I had to deflate the man's pomposity to find one significant clue.' The clue being Mortimer's remark concerning the tip-toe marks that Sir Charles, the latest victim of the curse, made as he returned to Baskerville Hall over the moor. 'But he wasn't tip-toeing Watson. He was running. Running for his life. Running in panic until he burst his heart.'

The heir of the Baskerville title, Sir Henry, is newly arrived from South Africa to take charge of the Dartmoor estate and Holmes visits his hotel to warn him of the possible dangers that await on the moor. While arranging for Watson to accompany the baronet down to Dartmoor, a tarantula spider slowly emerges from a boot Sir Henry is holding. The next tense moments are in the true Hammer horror mould. As Holmes bids Baskerville to keep still, the spider slowly clambers up his arm to his neck where it pauses. Holmes raises his cane and apparently only in the nick of time knocks the spider to the floor and crushes it.

This incident prompts the detective to utter this truly Sherlockian warning: 'The powers of evil can take many forms. Remember that, Sir Henry, when you are at Baskerville Hall. Do as the legend tells and avoid the moor when the forces of darkness are exalted.'

So Watson goes off with Sir Henry to Baskerville Hall. The film then follows the novel closely with Holmes making his surprise reappearance later on the moor. Surprise, that is, for Watson and for those moviegoers who are unfamiliar with the book.

Once back in the mainstream of the action Holmes carries out his investigations vigorously. 'There is more evil around us here, than I have ever encountered before,' he tells Watson. His trail leads him out of the confines of the Conan Doyle plot again and down a disused tin mine. When asked by Stapleton (Ewen Solon) what he expects to find down there, Holmes replies cryptically: 'Bones, perhaps'.

While venturing alone through a mine passage, one of the old trucks is set in motion by an unseen hand and smashes into the supporting timbers, bringing the roof down and apparently trapping the detective. After an unsuccessful attempt by Watson, Mortimer, Stapleton and a servant to dig through the rock blocking the shaft, they make their way back to the pony cart to find Holmes sitting there: 'When the general applause has died down, I wonder if we could go back to the Hall. I've hurt my leg; I'm cold and I'm hungry.' He later confides to Watson that he would not have ventured down the mine if he had not known there were a number of entrances to it.

The only other major deviation from Doyle is the relationship of Stapleton and his daughter (his sister in the book), renamed Cecile (Marla Landi). She is as much a part of the Hound plot as Stapleton. Indeed it is she who finally lures Sir Henry on to the moor at night. 'I too am a Baskerville, descended from Sir Hugo, descended from those who died in poverty while you scum ruled the moor. We've waited and prayed for this moment my father and I, now our time is come – and yours. The curse of the hound is on you,' she screams as her father lets loose the hound.

It is Holmes's injured leg and not the mist that delays him in dealing with the hound, which turns on Stapleton killing him before being in turn destroyed by Holmes. Cecile runs out on to the moor to be engulfed by the 'great Grimpen Mire'.

Sherlock Holmes (Peter Cushing) points out to Watson (André Morell) a significant clue to the identity of the murderer in *The Hound of the Baskervilles* (1959). *Hammer Film Productions Ltd*

Holmes shows the shaken baronet the dead hound. 'There is nothing to fear now. They used this mask to make it look more terrifying. It was starved for weeks; kept down the mine 'til the time was ripe then given the scent.'

Back safely in Baker Street over tea, served presumably by Mrs Hudson whom, sadly, we never see, Watson asks Holmes: 'When did you suspect the truth about this case? That the hound was a real dog and not just a legendary myth?'

'When Sir Henry complained of a missing boot, that put me on the scent as it were.'

'As early as that? Incredible.'

'Elementary, my dear Watson. Elementary.'

And so ends Hammer's *Hound*.

As with all Hammer productions, the sets and costumes are of the highest quality although it is a pity that there are no London exteriors, as in the 1939 version, to give a real sense of period. However, the moor exteriors are highly effective, fitting Doyle's description exactly: 'There rose ever dark against the evening sky, the long gloomy curve of the moor broken by the jagged and

Holmes shows Watson and the dishevelled Sir Henry Baskerville (Christopher Lee) the 'missing boot' which was used to give the hound the scent in *The Hound of the Baskervilles* (1959). *Hammer Film Productions Ltd*

sinister hills'. Surprisingly enough the film was not shot on Dartmoor but just outside London around Frenchman Ponds way. There are quite a few heights there and it closely resembles the dark barren emptiness of Dartmoor.

The biggest disappointment in the film is the appearance of the Hound itself. Determined to inject as much horror into the story as possible, Hammer, unlike Fox, emphasised the horrific elements of the hound so that when it finally appeared it was a marked anti-climax. However, presenting the hound had been a problem and ironically Terence Fisher, the director, stated in an interview: 'The dog was one of the kindest and loveliest dogs around. In fact for a lot of the close cutting work we used an artificial head and kept pushing it into various actors' faces.'

Terence Fisher, whose work for Hammer spans both the Frankenstein and Dracula series, holds an ambiguous position in the film world. While the more serious critics tend to regard his work as pedestrian and catchpenny, he is at the same time regarded as the doyen of contemporary fantasy film directors by devotees of such films. His work on the *Hound*, touches neither the highs or the lows; it is strong, competent storytelling at its unimaginative best. He does, however, with the aid of Jack Asher's photography and James Bernard's music, manage to inject into some of the moorland scenes, particularly those in the ruined abbey, a feeling of gothic menace.

Much to the disappointment of the Hammer people and despite their efforts to inject horror into a Holmes story, the film only received an 'A' certificate and not an 'X' which they saw as a surety of success. But as Terence Fisher remarked: '*Baskervilles* wasn't a horror film, but an adventure film.'

The twenty-year gap makes comparisons between this and the 1939 version unfair, each film having its own faults and merits, although the Fox film is superior in its greater sense of period and the opportunities it allows the detective to make his deductions.

Hammer's *Hound* was released in May 1959 and received mixed reviews. Margaret Hinxman, in a particularly insensitive review in *Picturegoer*, wrote: '. . . less of a thriller than a flamboyant period caricature, acted out in eye popping Sweeney Todd style, the film fails to grip', although she did admit it was 'produced with atmospheric flair'. Derek Conrad wrote in *Films and Filming*:

> This is one Hammer film that cannot be criticised for lack of taste. Perhaps they are still obsessed with bright red blood, but in *The Hound of the Baskervilles* they manage to suppress any wild desires they may have had to bathe artists and sets in it.
>
> Here is a good story told with as few gory frills as possible. This Conan Doyle – Sherlock Holmes opus is plausible but, oddly enough without suspense that would seem built-in on every page. The blame must be shared equally between director, screenwriter and editor. Instead of parallel action

(which is surely the fundamental rule of the suspense build up) the story-line goes from incident A to incident B without the slightest deviation . . . not even the whiff of a red herring.

On the subject of the screenplay *Variety* had different views:

> Peter Bryan's screenplay and dialogue is custom made for Holmes and Watson and handles the suspense and dramatic high spots well. Some of the settings are a shade stagey but Jack Asher's camera helps to build up the dark gloom of Dartmoor.

Sir Henry Baskerville was played by Christopher Lee, who must surely have been second on the casting director's short-list for the part of Holmes. In fact Lee did eventually play Holmes, but more of that later.

There can be little doubt that André Morell's performance as Watson must be the definitive one. Played with great sincerity and without any of the petulant buffoonery of Bruce and his impersonators, Morell's Watson comes closest to the image of the character that Conan Doyle's writings create. When asked about his portrayal of Watson in an interview, Morell said:

> Terence Fisher and Anthony Hinds (the producer) agreed not to do Watson as a comic character. Conan Doyle, after all, felt that Watson was a doctor and not an idiot as he was often made out to be. I deliberately avoided seeing Nigel Bruce, although he was very good – I just didn't want him to influence my acting of the part.

Surprisingly *The Hound of the Baskervilles* did not grip the audience and was a disappointment at the box office, causing Hammer to drop plans for further Conan Doyle thrillers. Of course the success or failure of any version of this Holmes story rests squarely on the shoulders of the actor who plays the famous detective. In this respect Hammer had a winner, for it was Peter Cushing who was, as billed in the trailer, 'the new and exciting Sherlock Holmes'.

Chapter 11

The Authentic Holmes

AS William Gillette was Holmes to pre-war theatre audiences, and Rathbone was Holmes to the wartime moviegoers, Peter Cushing has emerged as the Sherlock Holmes of the post-war years. As he himself says: 'I've played Baron Frankenstein and Professor Van Helsing many, many times, but I'm far better known to the public as Sherlock Holmes and I've only played him once in a film.'

Peter Cushing was born in Kenley, Surrey, in 1913. On leaving school he began work as a surveyor's assistant at the Coulsden and Purley Urban District Council. The job was his father's idea, for young Peter had ambitions to become an actor, but this profession was regarded as rather frivolous by his parents.

Cushing openly admits that up to the age of twenty he spoke English carelessly and indistinctly. He took an intensive course in speech training until he eradicated his major speech failings.

His overwhelming desire to act made him restless in his clerical duties and he tried to gain acceptance with various repertory companies. 'I used to take *The Stage* and answer advertisements in there. I tried for so long with my own name without success, that I thought a change of name might help. I was in the throes of first love at the time and the word darling was naturally used an awful lot, so I thought I'll call myself Peter Ling. Cut out the "dar" bit you see. So I sent a whole lot of letters to repertory companies saying,

"Here I am. What about it?" or words to that effect. But I soon changed my name back to Peter Cushing because I got a letter back from one of them saying, "I don't think there's much scope for Chinese actors in the repertory business".'

After bombarding Bill Fraser, who then ran the Connaught repertory company in Worthing, with letters asking for a job, he eventually received a reply which said 'Please come back and see me.' Overjoyed, Cushing quickly presented himself to Fraser who, on hearing his name, said, 'Oh I'm so glad you've turned up. It was just to ask you, please don't keep on writing to me because I've got so much else to do without answering all these letters.' Cushing broke down at this news, and Fraser, taking pity on the young aspiring actor, put him on the stage that very night, with a salary of fifteen shillings a week. The sheer hard work of repertory acting and the meagre financial rewards it brought did not daunt him. He was more than ever convinced that his decision to become an actor was the right one.

After four or five years in rep, he decided to chance his luck in Hollywood: 'I always wanted to go where Tom Mix lived'. Although totally unknown when he arrived in Hollywood, which was then in its heyday, with good bluffing and even better luck he managed to meet the director, James Whale, who was about to begin shooting *The Man in the Iron Mask*, in which Louis Hayward was to play twins – 'a good brother and an evil brother'. Whale was looking for someone to play opposite him to give Hayward something to play against. Cushing got the job.

'I played the good brother, while Louis Hayward played the bad and vice versa. Then the film was literally cut in the middle, my two lots were thrown away and Louis Hayward's were stuck together and there he was talking to himself.

'I was quite dreadful, because I was allowed to go and see the rushes, and I nearly fainted on the spot when I saw myself for the first time. I had a dreadful voice and I was as round as a dumpling. But as the weeks went by, it did improve a little and indeed they were very pleased with me and gave me this part of my own. I got on a horse and came rushing up and said "The King wants to see you".'

Cushing had little more to say in his next movie, *A Chump at Oxford*, a Laurel and Hardy comedy made at the Hal Roach studio. This feature is constantly turning up on television and it is interesting trying to spot Peter Cushing. Ironically *A Chump at Oxford* was made at the same time that Rathbone's *The Hound of the Baskervilles* was being filmed at the Fox studios, but in 1939 Peter Cushing was a long way from playing Holmes.

In 1941 Cushing made *Vigil in the Night*. The film starred Brian Aherne and Carol Lombard, but Cushing had a role which 'was virtually the second male lead'.

By this time war had broken out and Cushing wanted to come home.

Almost penniless, it took him eighteen months to get to England during which time he had a variety of jobs and had been arrested as a German spy. Once back in England an ear complaint prevented his admission into an active branch of the services, and so he began to work with the Entertainments National Service Association: ENSA known affectionately by the forces as 'Every Night Something Awful'. Shortly after joining ENSA 'the most important thing in my life happened, I met my wife Helen. I met her, of all romantic places for two actors to meet, outside the Theatre Royal Drury Lane stage door'. Helen died in 1971, leaving Cushing with an aura of sadness which seems unlikely to pass.

The forties was a lean time for the Cushings, although Peter made various theatre appearances and an Old Vic tour of Australia and New Zealand. His only film appearance was as Osric in Olivier's *Hamlet* in 1948.

As the fifties dawned, television began to catch on, and a television set came high on the list of domestic priorities in most homes. As a result more and more people were staying away from the cinema to view at home. At this time Peter Cushing became very active in television. 'I did three years solid television. I seemed to do nothing but plays then, wonderful plays.' His performance in one of these plays, an adaptation of George Orwell's *1984*, won him the Best Actor Award from the Television Guild.

Despite his success in television, Cushing was still very keen to get into films, 'because films were the things I always wanted to do'. So when he saw an advertisement in *The Stage* saying that Hammer films were looking for an actor to play Baron Frankenstein in a new film to be made, Cushing told his agent he was interested in playing the part. Hammer, it turned out, were only too delighted to have him play the title role in *The Curse of Frankenstein*, and the success of that film ensured that Cushing's future lay in films. Peter Cushing's reputation grew with Hammer's, and they used him as often as they could, and indeed it was not until well into the sixties that Cushing moved far from the Hammer stable, and even today he is the actor most used by the studio.

After completing the first of the many of the Frankenstein sequels, *The Revenge of Frankenstein* in 1958, he was handed the shooting script of *The Hound of the Baskervilles*, and was faced with the proposition of playing Sherlock Holmes. 'Many people had said you ought to play Holmes because you look rather like him, and I'd always considered it a jolly good part to play, and when I was offered the part I was absolutely thrilled. It's such a marvellous opportunity when you've got so much detail from the author to base your character upon.'

From childhood Cushing had been aware of the character of Sherlock Holmes. 'An uncle of mine was an absolute devotee of the Holmes stories, and I always remember him telling of a friend of his who had been accused of molesting a lady in a train. As a child I remember my uncle saying he proved the lady was telling a lie, rather like Sherlock Holmes. This man called the

guard along and said this lady has accused me of molesting her and it's absolutely impossible, look at my cigar, and it had about half an inch of ash on it. And I thought what an extraordinary man Sherlock Holmes must be, and eventually I read all the stories and thought they were wonderful.' And so Peter Cushing grew up to be a Holmes aficionado. Today he owns over sixty books on the subject including copies of the original *Strand* magazines.

Cushing approached the role with a meticulous enthusiasm. Always considering Conan Doyle to be the ultimate authority on Holmes, he carefully reread *The Hound of the Baskervilles* in order to present an authentic portrayal of Holmes. 'I tried to get as many of Holmes's mannerisms into the film as possible.'

In an interview I mentioned the disappointing appearance of the hound in the film and Peter Cushing recalled that its presentation was a problematic affair. 'They got a little boy and a little taller boy wearing suits exactly the same as Christopher Lee and myself were wearing as Holmes and Baskerville. They built a set the size of these children and put this dog in so it looked huge. And that's just what it looked like – two small children dressed up, a big dog and a small set. Of course they couldn't use it because it looked ludicrous. I don't know what the answer is because no dog will take make-up, it's trying to get it off all the time.' This proved so when Hammer attempted to make the dog glow: 'it just licked the make-up off'.

It is perhaps a pity that Hammer were obliged to concentrate on the horrific aspect of the dog for they were never able to match up to Doyle's description:

> A hound it was, an enormous coal-black hound, but not such a hound as mortal eyes have ever seen. Fire burst from its open mouth. Its eyes glowed with a smouldering glare, its muzzle and hackles and dewlap were outlined in flicking flame. Never in the delirious dream of a disordered brain could anything more savage, more appalling, more hellish, be conceived than that dark form and savage face which broke upon us out of the wall of fog.

Although neither Peter Bryan nor Hammer consulted Cushing during the preparation of the screenplay, he was able to inject some authentic Doyle touches once filming had started. A case in point is Holmes's reply to Dr Mortimer's boast concerning his generosity in the matter of fees. Cushing recalls, 'They had some line which was absolutely wrong, so I asked "Why can't we use one that Holmes actually said?" And so he used a line from the story *The Bridge:* "My professional charges are upon a fixed scale. I do not vary them, save when I remit them altogether".'

The Sherlock Holmes society voted Cushing's portrayal of Holmes as

Peter Cushing as Sherlock Holmes in the television version of *The Dancing Men* **(1968).**
Copyright © BBC

second only to Eille Norwood's, which, although an incongrous comparison, shows the respect they had for Cushing's work. Reviews, in general, with one or two exceptions, were in favour of the Cushing version. *Variety* in particular was effusive: 'Although everyone has his own idea of Sherlock Holmes, it is difficult to fault the performance of Peter Cushing'. *Films and Filming* noted that Peter Cushing appeared 'madly athletic' in comparison with the Rathbone Holmes. Ironically William K. Everson in his book, *The Detective in Film* thinks the reverse: 'as a man of action . . . he inspired little confidence'. Comments were also made about Cushing's build, for he is shorter and slighter than Conan Doyle's creation, but to me he overcomes the lack of size by the intelligence of his performance.

Peter Cushing never portrayed Holmes again for the cinema, but he did continue to play Professor van Helsing, the vampire expert and Dracula's arch enemy. Peter Cushing senses an affinity of spirit between these two characters. 'I think they have the same mental approach. Van Helsing has a great knowledge of vampires and is the essence of absolute good, and Dracula is the essence of absolute evil. And in a way old Holmes is the same. Moriarty was the arch

Peter Cushing and Nigel Stock (Dr Watson) in a scene from the television version of *Black Peter* (1968). *Copyright © BBC*

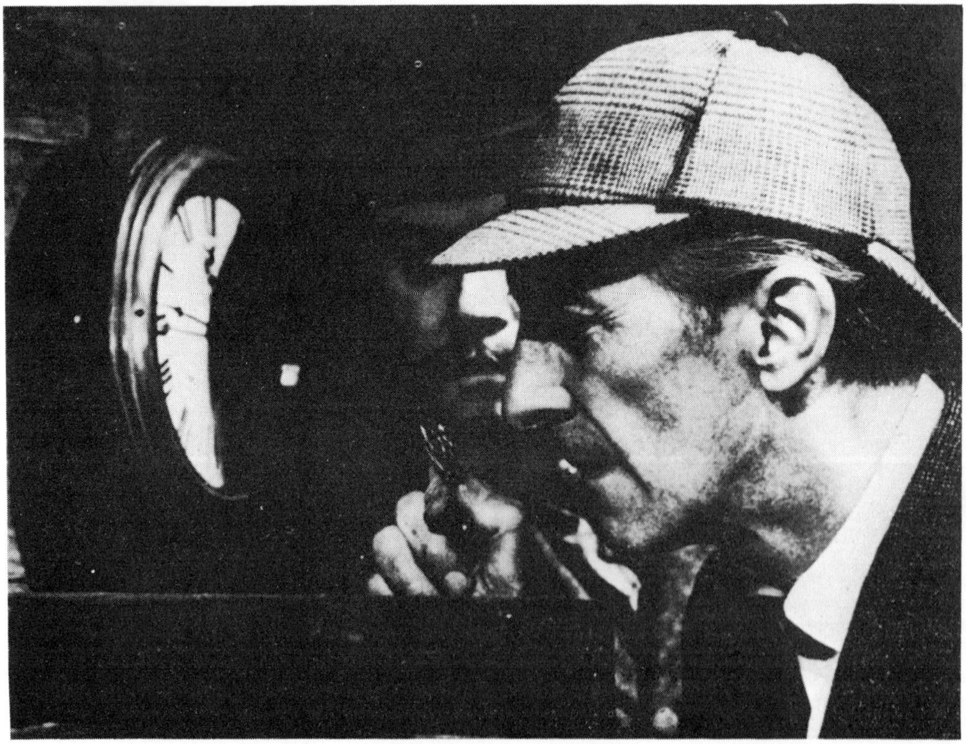

villain. Holmes was doing detective work as a private detective, but all his work was for the good of humanity in general.'

In recent years, Hammer, in an attempt to find new facets of the Dracula saga, have updated the Transylvanian fiend, placing him in modern London settings (*Dracula A.D. '72, The Satanic Rites of Dracula*) and Cushing, who plays Van Helsing's grandson in the films, feels that in general this updating 'came off', but that a similar updating treatment of Holmes would be wrong. 'There's no point. You might as well alter the name to Joe Smith and do it as a detective, but not as Sherlock Holmes. I think when such a wonderful atmosphere and character have been created by the author, it's an awful pity to bring it up to date. You've got aeroplanes and too many telephones and the fact was Holmes had nothing to work on but his incredible brain.'

What then did he think of the modern Rathbone Holmes films? 'I think I saw them all, and I loved them, although I never care for anything to be updated unless it is so in the books. But I think you must accept them of the time in which they were made because so much progress has been made in the actual way of making films you can't compare them with today's films. But as far as performance is concerned, I think he was absolutely super.'

But even so, for Peter Cushing the most impressive Holmes is Arthur Wontner: 'He to me was the one who looked most like the Paget drawings'.

Peter Cushing did play Holmes ten years later. However this time it was for the television screen. The series of sixteen programmes (fifteen stories with *The Hound of the Baskervilles* dramatised in two parts) was to have been the most ambitious and costly series devoted to the famous detective. At the onset the BBC considered such actors as Peter Ustinov, George Sanders and Orson Welles to play some of the villains. This plan never materialised.

The BBC handout at the time said this of the series:

> What is new in this series is the basic approach – a daring realisation of the lurking horror and callous savagery of Victorian crime, especially sexual crime. Here is the recreation of the Victorian half world of brutal males and the furtive innocent they dominate; of evil hearted servants scheming and embracing below stairs; of murder, mayhem and the macabre as the hansom cab once again sets out with Dr Watson and his debonair, eccentric and uncannily observant friend – Mr Sherlock Holmes.

Very commendable, but hardly a new approach, for all such details are to be found in the Conan Doyle canon.

The series turned out to be a curate's egg, with some of the stories suffering from the padding required to fill the fifty-minute time slot. Peter Cushing found, for personal reasons, he was less than happy with the series. 'We had been promised ten days to do each one of those sixteen episodes. Now that's enough so long as you have got the scripts beforehand, because I never go to anything unless I know it backwards, then I can change things as I go along. We got the scripts alright, but for each of the sixteen episodes, there were filmed inserts and the BBC had not made allowances for the English weather. By the time we got half way through the series, the series was already being shown, so we had to catch up and in the end we were doing them in three days. Whenever I see some of these, they upset me terribly, because it wasn't Peter Cushing doing his best as Sherlock Holmes, it was Peter Cushing looking relieved that he had remembered what to say and said it.'

Nevertheless the series had great merit, and was imbued with a reverential concern for presenting the stories in the true Doyle manner. This was mainly due to Peter Cushing's considered and intelligent portrayal of Holmes, and his efforts to create a true Holmesian authenticity. His preparation for the series was meticulous: 'I re-read all the stories in detail. There are so many facets of Holmes that you had to be careful that Doyle had not contradicted himself. For example his attitude to the country. On one occasion Holmes hates the country because nothing happens there, then he absolutely contradicts himself and says far worse things happen in the country.' He found dialogue phrases in the scripts that were too modern for the Victorian era and asked if they might be changed. He also made sure that as Holmes he never uttered the deathless phrase 'Elementary, my dear Watson', 'because it's not true – he never said the two together'.

At one of the production conferences Cushing made another request, this time regarding the appearance of Holmes. 'I said that just as one associates Tenniel's drawings with Alice in Wonderland, so with Holmes you associate so much Paget; although there have been other illustrators, he was the one. So, as I've got all the original *Strand* magazines showing what they wore in each story, could we dress each one as per the illustrations.' The BBC agreed, and in doing so they exploded the myth of Holmes's Inverness cape: 'It's not an Inverness cape in the drawings, it's a long overcoat with a hood and we had that coat made with the hood.'

The colour of Holmes's dressing-gowns as stated in the stories were carefully copied: the plum, the grey and the famous 'mouse' coloured one. Holmes's pipes also were meticulously catalogued and were made by the famous pipemakers, Charatars, in Jermyn Street, London. Cushing quite rightly rejected the Meerschaum, which was a William Gillette innovation and never referred to in the canon. 'The pipes are very well described and the reason why he smokes them: his favourite was the dirty old black clay pipe that "ponged" the study out; that was his great one for thinking. Then he had a long cherrywood for tranquility. Although I never had a Meerschaum, I did have a little bent one, but that was alright.'

Cushing recalls how these attempts at authenticity did not please all the viewers: 'The very first story to be shown was *The Hound of the Baskervilles* in which Holmes was dressed nearly all the time in the conventional way of the time which was frock coat and a top hat. Letters poured into the BBC saying "Why on earth do you want to dress Holmes and Watson like a couple of undertakers?" You see people only think of Holmes in a deerstalker, but in those days they were much more clothes conscious: you had country clothes and you had town clothes, and you wore them as such. And you notice that Holmes only wore his deerstalker when he was off in the country or when he came up from the country and was crossing from Victoria or whichever station to Baker Street.'

Cushing and Stock in a publicity still for the television series *Sherlock Holmes* **(1968).**
Copyright © BBC

The television version of *The Hound of the Baskervilles* was in fact the first time that Conan Doyle's tale of the spectral hound had actually been filmed on Dartmoor. However, because the story was shown in two parts and followed the novel almost to the letter it failed to grip as well as Hammer's *Hound*. Peter Cushing himself is happier with the film version: 'I prefer filming anyway and I think, with any luck, you can get a little nearer a certain perfection than you can in any other medium'.

Watson in the television series was played by the excellent actor Nigel Stock and although he presented the good doctor as an affectionate character, his portrayal was firmly in the Nigel Bruce mould. As a result Stock's performances, to some extent, were out of keeping with the authentic ambiance of the rest of the series.

In talking to Peter Cushing it becomes apparent that his portrayal of Sherlock Holmes is a labour of love. As an actor he commits himself totally

Peter Cushing as Sherlock Holmes scanning the sweep of the moors in the television version of *The Hound of the Baskervilles* (1968). **This was the first production to use actual Dartmoor locations.** *Copyright © BBC*

to every role he plays, but with Holmes he naturally employs an added dimension of interest because he so loves the character and the stories: 'I love them all. It's the atmosphere I love so much, and they've all got that. I love the way they start: it was always foggy and there were these equinoxal gales.' He reads the stories, not just as background reading to his performance as Holmes, but also 'purely for pleasure'.

With his gaunt features, high forehead and piercing blue eyes, Peter Cushing remains the thinking man's Holmes, who is very aware of Conan Doyle's place in the creation of the legend and who always goes 'back to the source' in his efforts to present the authentic Sherlock Holmes.

Earlier I wrote that I believed Basil Rathbone to be the ideal Holmes and in so many ways he is, but if I may paraphrase Shelley – if Rathbone comes can Cushing be far behind?

Chapter 12

Sherlock in the Sixties

THE Sixties brought a wind of change in the cinema and permissiveness raised its head. From the almost naïve self-conscious flashes of bosom and veiled references to sexual intercourse of the early sixties, we moved to flaunted full frontals and explicit sexual simulation of the late sixties and seventies.

In the climate of change and greater sexual freedom in the cinema, the character of the hero also inevitably changed. In the forefront of this attack was James Bond. Ian Fleming's sexual athlete hero was first brought to the screen in 1962 in *Dr No*. So successful was the Bond series that the screen became deluged with carbon copies of Fleming's hero. James Bond is the complete antithesis of Sherlock Holmes: he is a gadget-toting, girl-seducing, sophisticated hero, who only seems to show any ingenuity in a brawl or a bed. And probably his most unforgiveable anti-Sherlockian trait is his immorality.

Of course James Bond is not the cause, but the effect. Suffice it to say that in a world of bosoms, beds and bad language Sherlock Holmes has no place, and so since the start of this permissiveness, Holmes has been very inactive in films. However, since the Hammer version of *The Hound of the Baskervilles* there have been several major films featuring the great detective and I shall be dealing with two of these in this chapter.

The first Holmes film of the sixties is one that few have seen, and those who have wish to forget it, including the director Terence Fisher: 'It's a film well worth left alone'. The failure of *Sherlock Holmes and the Deadly Necklace,* the film in question, seems to be a case of 'too many cooks'. The movie was a German/Italian/British/French co-production. 'The film', commented Christopher Lee, 'was a badly edited hodge podge of nonsense'.

In the planning stages the film looked as though it would be an impressive effort, with Christopher Lee starring as Holmes, and the excellent British character actor Thorley Walters as Watson. Terence Fisher was to direct. The screenplay was written by Curt Siodmak, whose other film credits include the horror classic *The Beast with Five Fingers.*

The film was originally intended to be an adaptation of *The Valley of Fear,* but in its final form it bore no resemblance to the original Conan Doyle tale and so was retitled *Sherlock Holmes and the Deadly Necklace* (*Sherlock Holmes und das Halsband des Todes*). Terence Fisher ended up sharing directing chores with Frank Witherstein. The movie was so inept that it was not until 1968 that it found theatrical release in England and in the United States it was shunted off directly into television playoff.

Christopher Lee has expressed regret at the film's missed chances:

> I think it was a pity, this film, in more ways than one. We should never have made it in Germany with German actors, although we had a British art director and a British director. It was a hodge podge of stories put together by the German producers, which ruined it. My portrayal of Holmes is, I think, one of the best things I've ever done because I tried to play him really as he was written, as a very intolerant, argumentative, difficult man, and I looked extraordinarily like him with the make-up. Everyone who's seen it said I was as like Holmes as any actor they've ever seen both in appearance and interpretation.

Whether in fact Lee makes a good Holmes or not is difficult to assess, for in the English version of the film his voice was dubbed by an odd, high-pitched, nasal one. One can only lament the film's unrealised potential.

The plot concerns the theft of a priceless necklace which is among the treasures discovered by a group of English and Egyptian archaeologists in a tomb believed to be that of Cleopatra. While the theft of the necklace baffles Scotland Yard a man arrives at Sherlock Holmes's rooms in Baker Street just in time to whisper a single word and make some curious flowing gestures with his hand before dying. Watson is puzzled, but Holmes quickly deduces that the man is referring to a dockland pub known as the 'Hare and Eagle'.

Holmes and Watson visit the pub where they overhear Professor Moriarty in conversation with a cohort. Later Holmes breaks into Moriarty's apartment

Thorley Walters (Dr Watson), Christopher Lee (Sherlock Holmes), Hans Nielson, and Senta Berger in a scene from *Sherlock Holmes and the Deadly Necklace* (1962). *CCC Film*

where he finds the necklace hidden in a sarcophagus. He hands this over to Inspector Cooper (Hans Nielson) who is to guard it until the public auction at which it is to be sold.

Holmes, realising that Moriarty will attempt to get the necklace back, disguises himself as a thug and repairs to the 'Hare and Eagle' where he gets himself recruited by Moriarty's henchman. While some of Moriarty's cronies force the police van transporting the necklace to stop over a manhole, Holmes and others of the gang come up from the sewers and steal the necklace.

After disposing of his colleagues, the master detective goes to the auction room with the necklace where Inspector Cooper is lamenting the loss.

Due to lack of evidence, Moriarty is allowed to go free, seemingly to pave the way for further such encounters with Holmes. These have never materialised.

Although *The Monthly Film Bulletin* thought that; 'apart from some startling anachronisms the period detail was on the whole nicely done', the film came in for some harsh criticism from the critics. Marjorie Bilbow summed up the general opinion with her comment in *Cinema and T.V. Today:* 'As a story woven around an unknown detective it would have been forgiveable, but classic characters demand more accurate handling than this.'

The year 1965 saw the release of the first 'X' certificate Sherlock Holmes feature. The certificate was awarded, it would appear, not for any horror content, but for the sexual elements implicit in the movie. The idea behind *A Study in Terror* was, to say the least, inspired – that of pitting the world's greatest detective against the world's most fiendish killer, Jack the Ripper. On reflection it seems strange that no one had considered bringing about this confrontation previously, for during the autumn of 1888, while the Ripper was committing the atrocities on prostitutes, Holmes was at the peak of his powers. At the same time that Whitechapel was ringing with cries of the unfortunate women, the great sleuth was working on the Baskerville Case. (Sherlockian experts disagree over the dating of Holmes's cases, but William S. Baring Gould in his 'biography' of the detective places the Baskerville case in the autumn of 1888.)

However, in 1965, Compton films brought to the screen this intriguing blend of fact and fiction under the title of *A Study in Terror*.

The film opens amid Jack the Ripper's reign of terror in London's East End, where already two street women have met gruesome deaths in the fog shrouded alleys of Whitechapel. But yet another prostitute is to die before the great detective becomes involved in the murders, and he does so in an unusual way. Holmes receives an anonymous package bearing a Whitechapel postmark. The package is found to contain a case of surgical instruments with the post mortem scalpel missing.

As Holmes scrutinises the case with his magnifying glass, Watson eagerly inquires if the case tells him anything. 'To start with, the obvious: these instruments belong to a medical man who has descended to hard times.'

'I would hardly call that obvious.'

'The instruments of one's trade [sic] are always the last things to be pawned.'

'But how do you know they were pawned?' asks the good doctor, without flinching in the least at his companion's reference to the medical profession as a 'trade'.

'Observe this speck of white,' continues Holmes, pointing to one of the instruments, 'silver polish. No surgeon would ever clean his instruments with silver polish. They've been treated like common cutlery by someone concerned only with their appearance. This is substantiated by these chalk marks. They relate to the pawn ticket number.'

'They were stolen from a doctor and then pawned', suggests Watson.

'If the pawnbroker had thought they were stolen he would never have displayed them in a window. The shop faces south in a narrow street, and business is bad. I should also add that the pawnbroker is a foreigner . . .'

'I cannot see . . .' begins Watson but Holmes quickly interrupts him.

'On the contrary, you see everything, but observe nothing. Observe how the material has faded here. The sun has touched the inside of the case only when at its height and able to shine over the roofs of the buildings opposite. Hence the shop is in a narrow street facing south. And business had to be bad for the case to remain undisturbed for so long.'

'But how can you possibly tell the pawnbroker was foreign?'

'The seven in the pledge number is crossed in the Continental manner.'

Sherlock Holmes (John Neville) and Dr Watson (Donald Houston) seem interested in the case of medical instruments in the possession of Lord Fairfax (John Fraser) in *A Study in Terror* (1965). *Compton-Cameo*

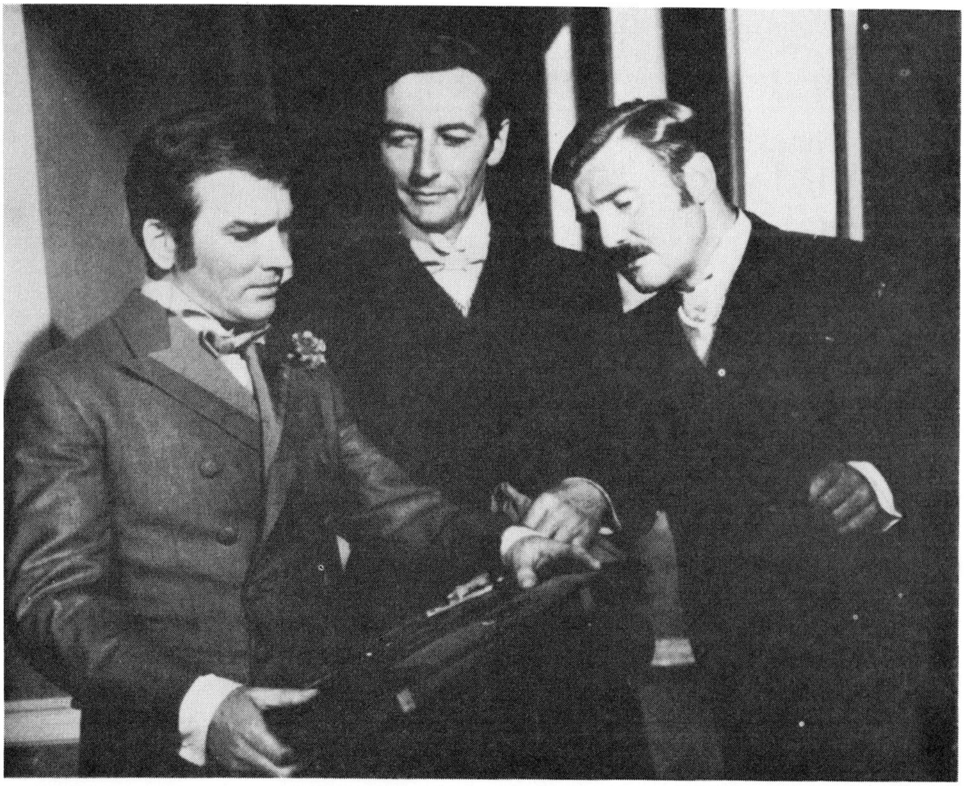

It would seem from this elaborate piece of deduction that Holmes is in fine form and that the screen writers have in their original dialogue caught the true flavour of Conan Doyle. However, this standard is not easily maintained and unfortunately the rest of the film does not match up to the fine exposition.

Holmes discovers under the felt lining in the lid of the box, the coat of arms of the Osbournes. Holmes and Watson visit the head of this noble family, the Duke of Shires (Barry Jones), who recognises the box of instruments as belonging to his eldest son Michael whom he has disowned. As they are being shown out Holmes bumps into the Duke's younger son, Lord Carfax (John Fraser), who confirms that the instruments belong to his brother Michael who disappeared shortly after graduating from the Sorbonne.

Holmes's next move is to seek out the Whitechapel pawnshop, which is found as he predicted in a narrow street facing south. Here he learns that the instruments were pawned by a woman calling herself Angela Osbourne. Her address was given as an East End hostel.

The detective learns that the hostel, which incorporates a soup kitchen and a small hospital, is run by Doctor Murray (Anthony Quayle) with the aid of his niece, Sally (Judi Dench) and is financed by Lord Carfax. Determined to find the whereabouts of Angela Osbourne, whom he believes is the key to

Insp Lestrade (Frank Finlay) and Sherlock Holmes (John Neville) watch Dr Murray (Anthony Quale) as he performs an autopsy on one of Jack the Ripper's victims in *A Study in Terror* (1965). *Compton-Cameo*

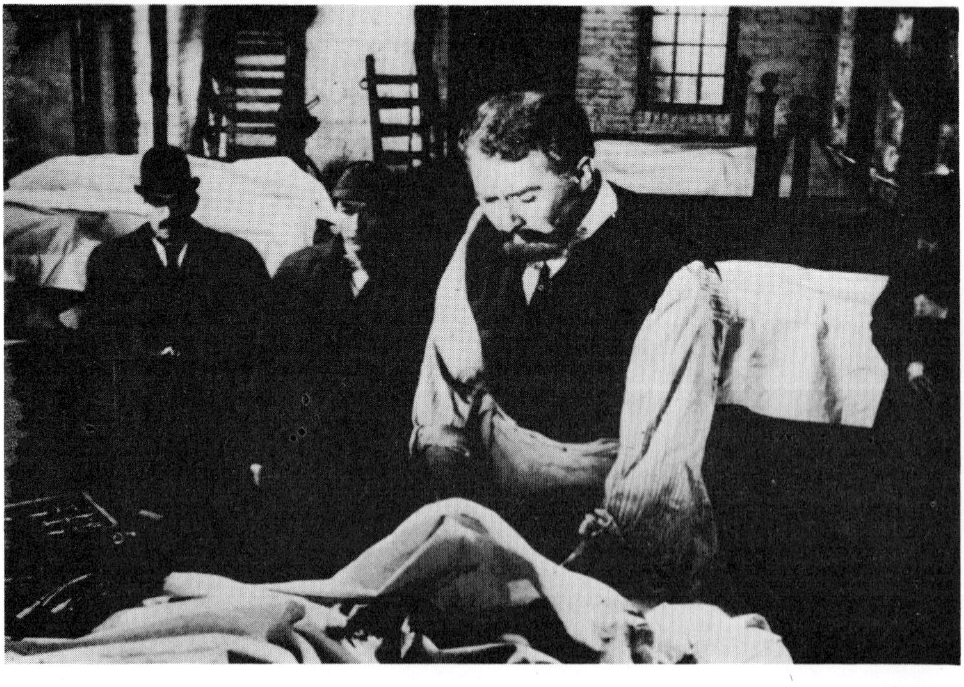

the Ripper murders, Holmes persuades Watson to go to the soup kitchen to make enquiries about this woman.

While Watson, acting on Holmes's instructions, makes a scene at the soup kitchen on being told by Dr Murray and Sally that they know nothing of the Osbourne woman, the detective, disguised as an old tramp, watches the proceedings keenly. After Watson's stormy exit, Sally leaves hurriedly trailed by the disguised Holmes.

He follows her to a small house nearby and on entering finds Lord Carfax. 'Don't you think you ought to tell me the whole story', suggests Holmes, throwing off his disguise. Carfax eventually agrees:

> 'I found that my brother had thrown up his studies in Paris and returned to England. For weeks I tried to find him. Then one night a man came to see me. He told me that Michael had married a prostitute.'
>
> 'Blackmail. He threatened to tell the papers?'
>
> 'He was far cleverer than that. He threatened to tell my father. He'd chosen his time well, my father had just suffered a severe heart attack that very week.'

Michael's whereabouts still remain unknown, but Lord Carfax reveals that the blackmailer is Max Steiner owner of the Angel and Crown tavern. Holmes confronts Steiner, when he visits the tavern:

> 'You know Angela Osbourne well, I take it.'
>
> 'How do you know that?' sneers Steiner.
>
> 'There had to be an accomplice in your blackmail.'
>
> 'Compensation I call it. I could have opened my mouth and collected from the press, or kept it shut and collected from Lord Carfax. I did the nobility of England a service, Mr Holmes. Lord Carfax compensates me for my loss of business with the newspapers.'

When Holmes asks where Angela Osbourne is now, Steiner shakes his head and says that she has disappeared from the face of the earth.

On leaving the tavern, Holmes and Watson are attacked by thugs but they survive the fray with the aid of Holmes's cane which conceals a short sword. 'Nothing like a piece of cold steel, eh Holmes?' grins Watson as their assailants beat a hasty retreat.

Dr Murray, aside from his duties at the hostel hospital, also acts as coroner for the police and performs autopsies on the murder victims. He sees the Ripper's activities as beneficial in bringing the attention of the authorities to the dreadful conditions that prevail in Whitechapel. As he tells a crowd at a meeting in this area:

> It's not the killings by a demented hand the world finds horrible. No, it's the murder by poverty; the murder by misery, the murder by hunger in Whitechapel. The cry of the starving, the moan of the sick. It is the social and moral crime that must be ended in Whitechapel.

The government, frightened by the political implications of the horrors of Whitechapel, officially seek Holmes's assistance in their investigations. Sherlock's brother Mycroft is instructed by the Prime Minister to enlist Holmes's services in order to bring Jack the Ripper to justice.

While Mycroft is engaged in persuading his brother to help the struggling government, Inspector Lestrade bursts into the Baker Street chambers with a letter written by the murderer:

> Dear Boss,
> I keep hearing that the police have caught me, but they won't fix me yet. I have to laugh when they look so clever and talk about being on the right track. I am down on whores, and won't rest until I do get buckled. I love my work and want to start again. My knife is nice and sharp. I want to get to work right away. Good luck.
> Yours truly,
> Jack the Ripper.

The letter is the precursor of another murder. Holmes with Lestrade visits Murray's hostel to view the body: 'What is your opinion of the knife work here Doctor? Does it not show surgical skill?' asks Holmes.

'Anyone with a modicum of medical training could have done it, yes,' agrees Murray.

'A medical student perhaps? It is true these murders are the work of a madman, but a madman with certain medical skills, considerable intelligence and education?'

Lestrade finds this claim preposterous. Holmes explains:

> Take that letter, the punctuation was exact. The grammar and syntax, though cleverly concealed, were the work of an educated man, and to a graphologist it was obvious that the writing was deliberately scrawled. We must not take the mask for the face!

The next night Holmes and Watson patrol the alleys of Whitechapel, but their presence does not prevent the Ripper striking again. However Holmes is close on his heels as he makes his getaway and the Ripper only just manages to elude the detective in Dr Murray's hostel. Holmes now confronts Murray who reluctantly admits he knows the whereabouts of Michael Osbourne. The doctor discloses that Michael Osbourne worked in the surgery with him. One

Mycroft Holmes (Robert Morley), Dr Watson (Donald Houston), Sherlock Holmes (John Neville) and Insp Lestrade (Frank Finlay) read a letter written by Jack the Ripper in *A Study in Terror* (1965). *Compton-Cameo*

night when Angela and Steiner had attempted to involve Osbourne in the plot to blackmail his father, a fight broke out in which an uncorked bottle of acid, intended for Michael, was thrown in Angela's face: 'Her angel face was a diabolical sight. I did the best I could for her. A week later Steiner took her away in a closed cab and I've not seen or heard from her since that day.'

'And Michael Osbourne?' prompts Holmes.

Murray leads him to a small room in the hostel where an inarticulate simpleton is seen cowering in a corner.

'You wanted Michael Osbourne – here he is', says Murray grimly. 'Whether it was Steiner's blows to the head, or whether his mind could suffer no more of the world his wife had shown him, I don't know, but this is how he's been since that night.'

'How could Lord Carfax allow his brother to remain here in that condition?'

'He doesn't know, Holmes. Not even his own brother could recognise that poor creature as Michael Osbourne.'

Holmes now realises that Steiner is Angela's lover and there is only one place where she can be hiding. He pieces together the remainder of the story when he confronts Angela Osbourne, horribly disfigured and leading an existence of total seclusion in a single room above the 'Angel and Crown'. Holmes tells her that he knows it was she who sent him the case of surgical instruments in an attempt to interest him in the Ripper murders.

Angela Osbourne presents a different picture of Michael. 'To Dr Murray, Michael was a saint, but to me Michael was a man who tired easily. He seemed unbalanced at times. He couldn't take the discipline of medical study. It was the same with marriage. He quickly tired of me and sent me back to work on the streets.' She purports it was Michael who was behind the blackmail scheme and that it was he who deliberately threw the acid into her face when she told him she was leaving him for Steiner. At this Angela reveals her gruesome scarred face: 'I'm not your killer. As you can see I'm incapable of stepping out into the street.'

The next day Holmes and Watson, with Lord Carfax, take the demented Michael Osbourne to his family home. After their task is completed, the detective confides to Watson that the last act of Jack the Ripper is about to commence.

That night the Ripper slips into Angela's room and is about to stab her while she lies asleep when Holmes steps from the shadows with a greeting: 'Good Evening Lord Carfax!' The Ripper attacks Holmes and in the ensuing struggle an oil lamp is overturned starting a fire which engulfs the Ripper along with Angela and Steiner. Holmes, however, escapes unharmed: 'You know my methods, Watson. I am known to be indestructable.'

There just remains the familiar post mortem scene where Watson, eyebrows raised, presses Holmes into an explanation of the whole case and how he knew Lord Carfax was Jack the Ripper.

> 'His medical knowledge. When I dropped the case of instruments in his father's house, he picked it up. You remember that Watson? Did you not notice that he immediately put the instruments in their right niches. How odd, I thought. How interesting. A layman might ponder for a moment, but Carfax did not hesitate.'
>
> 'But if that's all you have to go on, isn't it an obvious fact that . . .'
>
> 'There's nothing more deceptive than an obvious fact, Watson. But what was most obvious and revealing was the letter. The writer described his murders as his work – "I love my work", "I want to get to work right away". If his gruesome activity was, as he said it was, his work, he was obviously a man of means who had no need of ordinary employment. Dr Murray who works very hard would have written, perhaps, "pastime". I ruled out Murray.'
>
> 'You make it sound so simple,' mutters Watson.

'So it was,' continues the smug detective, 'when I investigated the Osbourne family I found insanity through four generations. Carfax's reason hung on a thread. That his brother should put the name of Osbourne to a common prostitute, and that she should carry that name to the street corners of Whitechapel, broke that thread. Carfax was protecting, insanely, the family name. He'd never seen Angela, but it seemed logical to him, mad to us, that he could kill her by a process of elimination. He searched for her with his knife from one prostitute to the next.'

'But Lestrade – the police?'

'Lestrade and the police do not know the identity of Jack the Ripper. No useful purpose will be served by disclosing his identity now. The Osbourne family have suffered enough as it is. Lestrade has his three buckets of ash, but we will keep the name.'

This rather contrived and unconvincing exposition brings the film to its close. The script certainly has its merits. It is commendable, for instance, in the way in which the writers, Donald and Derek Ford, managed to blend the authentic details of the Ripper murders, including the letter, with the fictitious plot. But in general its convoluted and contrived path was detrimental to the effectiveness of the film. One critic was prompted to write: 'All sink in a thick plot.'

The producers of the film wished to present the detective in a new light. They said that he was no longer to be the old fuddy duddy Holmes, as the public had tended to classify him in the past: 'he is now way out and with it'. Even if we accept their original premise it is a very dangerous thing to tamper with legendary characters. The last thing Conan Doyle's Holmes would wish to be is 'with it'.

The experiment does not come off. Holmes emerges without the mystic authority and towering intellectualism that the character demands. Sherlock Holmes was played by John Neville making one of his rare film appearances. Of his approach to the character he said:

> I'd always felt, having seen Sherlock Holmes in my childhood, that he was perhaps rather more stiff-backed, stuffy, arrogant and conceited than he need be. I was worried about his relationship with Dr Watson. I felt that he'd often been treated as an old duffer. I think there's a very warm relationship between them, even though Holmes often teases Watson. This was something that Donald Houston and I worked on, so that this relationship had a sort of fun about it and warmth, rather than Holmes just being arrogant and condescending to Watson.

Despite the skill and care of John Neville's performances, his Holmes remains only a vigorous caricature. Although possessing suitably gaunt features,

Neville's face and hairstyle were far too modern to be effective and erase the Paget-like images of Cushing and Rathbone. Neville scores most successfully in his handling of the dialogue, but this at times is so devoid of period feeling as to jar.

The relationship between Holmes and Watson (played by Donald Houston as a younger duffer) is never really established as Neville wished it to be. This is partly due to the interpretation of Watson by Donald Houston who had both feet firmly in the Nigel Bruce camp. One American critic said of Houston's performance: 'he has spiced the role with a blushing bashfulness reminiscent

John Neville, Robert Morley and Donald Houston in a scene from ***A Study in Terror*** (1965). *Compton-Cameo*

of the late great Oliver Hardy'. So many film makers seem compelled to present Holmes and Watson as a double act with Holmes as the straight man and Watson as the comedy relief. In doing this they fail to establish the essential relationship between the two men as portrayed in the books. Only once, in Hammer's *Hound,* due to André Morell's skilled underplaying and Peter Cushing's intelligent approach to the Holmes role, has this relationship been successfully transferred to the screen.

The cast of *A Study in Terror* also includes Frank Finlay who was suitably thick skulled and rat-faced as Inspector Lestrade. Robert Morley gives a pleasant performance in the cameo role of Sherlock's brother, Mycroft. Morley's rotund appearance fits exactly Conan Doyle's conception of the character: 'His body was absolutely corpulent, but his face, though massive, had preserved something of the sharpness of expression which was so remarkable in that of his brother'.

Not all the reviews of *A Study in Terror* were condemnatory. In America it was well received and regarded as a 'snappy, handsomely mounted production'. While in Britain, the film critic of the *Daily Worker* thought Neville made the best screen Sherlock yet.

Despite these sanguine reviews the film failed to impress at the box office, and it did in fact sound the death knell of Compton films. As well as spending an above average amount on the production, they went all out in their promotional campaign, producing giant-sized press books and folders. It was to be the first in a series of new Holmes adventures authorised by the Conan Doyle estate, but its failure at the box office put an end to these exciting and ambitious plans.

Not only did the failure of *A Study in Terror* deny Holmes's fans further new adventures of the detective from Compton, but it revealed how risky a film subject Sherlock Holmes had become and as a result of this no film maker since has dared to make a straight Holmes movie.

Chapter 13

Wilder in Baker Street

BILLY Wilder belongs to that select band of directors which includes Alfred Hitchcock, William Wyler, Ken Russell and David Lean, whose names are familiar to the most desultory of moviegoers. The Wilder stamp on a movie is recognised as the stamp of quality, and although this Austro-Hungarian has more recently been concentrating on comedy, he has been responsible for some fine dramas.

Wilder's success lies in his total commitment to his films, for not only does he direct and produce, but he is also involved in the writing of them. It was as a writer that he first made his entry into films in 1930 with *People on Sunday*. Before he made his directional debut he worked on the screenplays of such thirties goodies as *Midnight*, *Ninotchka*, and *Ball of Fire*.

His first film as a director was *The Major and the Minor* in 1942 and within three years he had earned himself the Academy Award for *Lost Weekend*, a penetrating study of alcoholism. Wilder's film list fairly drips with gems including *Ace in the Hole, Sunset Boulevarde, The Seven Year Itch, Witness for the Prosecution, Some Like it Hot, One Two Three* and *The Apartment* (another Academy Award).

Although it would seem that Billy Wilder's forte is humour, his comedies show a skilful examination and understanding of the sensitive interplay involved in human relationships. Bearing this in mind it does not seem so unusual that he should turn his creative attention to the intriguing aspects of the relationship between Holmes and Watson.

Wilder began filming *The Private Life of Sherlock Holmes* at Pinewood Studios in the summer of 1969. The intention of the film was to 'fill in what Conan Doyle left out'. Like so many creative artists who become involved with the Holmes character, it was a labour of love – a visit to the shrine. He had read the Holmes tales in Germany as a boy and loved them ever since. 'We could have filmed one of the existing stories', he said, 'but that wasn't enough of a challenge. We want to explore the characters more and fill in the gaps'.

It became more obvious as Wilder talked about the production, that in filling gaps, he and fellow screenplay writer I.A.L. Diamond were involved in taking licence with the character. The film was to be a Holmes spoof, although Wilder professed:

> We're approaching the characters and the Baker Street atmosphere in a straightforward manner, with warm heartedness and good humour. I love the stories and the last thing I would want to do is guy them in any way. We hope to treat Holmes and Watson with respect but not reverence. There is a certain amount of natural humour, but the stories in our picture essentially show the relationships and friendship between the two men.

Wilder chose Robert Stephens, better known as a stage actor, for the lead. Strangely enough, Stephens, a childhood fan of the detective, was the original choice for the Holmes role in *A Study in Terror*. Colin Blakely, another actor more often seen on stage and the small screen than in films, was chosen to play Watson. Christopher Lee was given the role of Mycroft, thus making him the only actor to have played both the Holmes brothers.

Before shooting started Wilder presented the principle members of the cast with bound volumes of Baring Gould's *Annotated Sherlock Holmes* as gifts in order that they could immerse themselves in the atmosphere and background detail of their parts.

The film was one of Wilder's most extravagant productions involving a nineteen week schedule at Pinewood with six weeks' location at Inverness. During the location filming on the banks of Loch Ness, the Scottish Tourist Board trade index increased by about two hundred per cent, and many happy visitors went away hugging photographs they had taken of the Loch Ness monster, little realising it was one built especially for the film.

One of the most impressive sets ever erected at Pinewood was Alexander Trauner's *pièce de resistance* for the film – 150 yards of Baker Street with fully built up fronts and smaller buildings receding in perspective, shops dressed with authentic Victorian bric-a-brac, real cobblestones and some authentically beery pubs. When used, this set which took over four months to build, utilised a hundred extras in costume and nineteen horse-drawn carriages.

Even the smaller sets were impressive. The Baker Street living-room was incredibly detailed and authentic, thanks not only to the expertise of Trauner, but also Wilder's meticulous attention to detail. So authentic was this set that Adrian (son of Sir Arthur) Conan Doyle commented: 'If Sherlock Holmes were to visit this room he would immediately feel right at home – everything is exactly in its place – a brilliant recreation'.

It would seem that before the filming began, *The Private Life of Sherlock Holmes*, in the hands of such a talented director, cast and set designer, was all

Sherlock Holmes (Robert Stephens) and Dr Watson (Colin Blakely) arrive back at Baker Street to be greeted by Mrs Hudson (Irene Handl). The scene shows the impressive set specially constructed for *The Private Life of Sherlock Holmes* **(1970).**
Mirisch

set to be a winner. However something happened to it on its way to the cinema screen.

The original intention had been to present four stories within the framework of the film, but the finished product had only one mystery. Six weeks after filming began the script was unfinished and the planned three hour film emerged on release, with chunks cut out of it, at a mere two hours five minutes.

The pre-credits sequence reveals that in the vaults of a London bank lies a despatch box which belonged to Doctor Watson – the Doctor Watson. The instructions are that the box is not to be opened until fifty years after his death. Watson in voice-over explains:

> It contains certain mementoes of my association with a man who elevated the science of deduction into an art. In my life I have recorded some sixty cases demonstrating the singular gifts of my friend Mr Sherlock Holmes . . . but there were other adventures which, for reasons of discretion, I have decided to withhold from the public until this later date. They involve matters of a delicate and scandalous nature as will shortly become apparent.

And so with appetites whetted, Miklos Rozas' superb theme music rises to a climax and the elegant credits begin. From this preamble it seems apparent that we are in for some frank revelations concerning Holmes and his 'censored' cases.

The opening scene is beautifully conceived and it is one of the most effective of Holmes parodies. Its success lies in the lightness of touch in the playing and writing and is presented in such a way, that although the whole thing is tongue in cheek, one can sense a love and reverence for the character shining through.

Holmes and Watson have just returned to Baker Street after another successful case which, we are told, Holmes solved by measuring the depth to which the parsley had sunk in the butter on a hot day. 'I wish you'd give me a bit more warning when you come home unexpectedly,' cries Mrs Hudson, after giving Watson an affectionate hug. 'I would have roasted a goose, had some flowers for you.' 'My dear Mrs Hudson,' replies Holmes, 'criminals are as unpredictable as head colds. You never quite know when you're going to catch one.'

While she bustles off, Watson examines his mail, and exclaims:

> 'Here is an advance copy of the *Strand Magazine*. They've printed *The Red Headed League*. Would you like to see how I've treated it?'
>
> 'I can hardly wait. I am sure I shall find out all sorts of fascinating things about the case that I never knew before.'
>
> 'What d'you mean by that?' asks a petulant Watson.
>
> 'Oh, come now, Watson, you must admit you have a tendency to over-

romanticise. You have taken my simple exercises in logic and embellished them, embroidered them, exaggerated them . . .'

'I deny the accusation.'

'You have described me as six foot four, whereas I am barely six foot one.'

'A bit of poetic licence.'

'You have saddled me with this improbable costume, which the public now expects me to wear.'

'It was not my doing – blame it on the illustrator.'

'You have made me out to be a violin virtuoso: here's an invitation from the Liverpool Symphony to appear as soloist in the Mendelssohn Violin Concerto. The fact is, I could barely hold my own in the pit orchestra of a second rate music hall.'

'You're much too modest.'

'You've given the reader the distinct impression I'm a misogynist. Actually I don't dislike women: I merely distrust them. The twinkle in the eye and the arsenic in the soup.'

'It's these little touches that make you colourful.'

'Lurid is more like it. You've painted me as a hopeless dope addict, just because occasionally I take a five per cent solution of cocaine.'

'A seven per cent solution,' corrects the Doctor.

'Five per cent. Do you think I am not aware you've been diluting it behind my back?'

'As a doctor as well as your friend, I strongly disapprove of this insidious habit of yours.'

'My dear friend as well as my dear doctor, I only resort to narcotics when I am suffering from acute boredom. When there are no interesting cases to engage my mind. Look at this – an urgent appeal to find some missing midgets.'

Watson raises his eyebrows: 'Did you say midgets?'

'Mm, six of them. "The Tumbling Piccolos", an acrobatic act with some circus.' Holmes hands the letter to Watson who reads it quickly. 'Disappeared between London and Bristol. Don't you find that intriguing?'

'Extremely so. You see they're not only midgets but also anarchists.'

'Anarchists!'

'By now they will have been smuggled to Vienna as little girls in organdie pinafores. They are to greet the Czar of all the Russias when he arrives at the railway station. They will be carrying bouquets of flowers and concealed in each bouquet will be a bomb with a lit fuse.'

'D'you really think so?'

'Not at all. The circus owner offers me five pounds for my services. That's not even a pound a midget. So obviously he is a stingy blighter and the little chaps simply ran off to join another circus.'

'Sounded so promising.'

'There are no great crimes any more, Watson. The criminal class have lost all enterprise and originality. At best they commit some bungling villainy with a motive so transparent that even a Scotland Yard official can see through it.'

The whole scene is a joy and is so successful because it only just crosses the borderline between the authentic and the satirical, so that one can imagine Conan Doyle having written it in a mood of whimsy. This scene would hardly offend the most rigorous of Holmes purists, but alas the same cannot be said for the rest of the film. Its gradual decline can be plotted from the end of this scene.

Galled by inactivity, Holmes once more resorts to cocaine injections, while desultorially working on his monograph on cigarette ashes with aid of a machine, which, incorporating a bellows device, is able to 'smoke' as many as six cigarettes at once. When Mrs Hudson (played in true British boarding-house keeper fashion by the delightful Irene Handl) complains about the amount of smoke produced by the machine, Dr Watson explains to her Holmes's task. 'So far he has classified one hundred and forty different kinds of ashes.'

'All of which have wound up on my rug,' replies Mrs Hudson tersely.

Accepting with little enthusiasm a mysterious invitation to the visiting Russian Ballet, Holmes is invited backstage to meet the famous prima ballerina, Petrova. Her manager puts to Holmes a delicate proposition. He offers Holmes a Stradivarius violin in return for his services. But not his detective services – he is asked to provide Madam Petrova with a child. She, apparently, has chosen Holmes to be the father of her child, because his intellectual qualities are equal to her own vaunted beauty.

'This is all very flattering, but surely there are other men, better men?' gabbles Holmes, visibly nonplussed. The secretary assures Holmes that he was not the first choice. 'We considered our Russian writer, Tolstoy.'

'That's more like it,' beams the detective, 'the man's a genius.'

'Too old. Then we considered the philosopher Nietzsche.'

'A first rate mind.'

'Too German. Then we considered Tchaikovsky.'

'You couldn't go wrong with Tchaikovsky.'

'We could and we did. It was a catastophe.'

'Why?'

'Because Tchaikovsky . . . how shall I put it? Women are not his glass of tea.'

Holmes is dismayed and apparently trapped as Madame Petrova's final choice. Eventually he confesses that he is not a free man.

'But you are a bachelor,' cries the secretary.

'A bachelor, living with another bachelor for the last five years. Five very happy years.'

'What is it you are trying to tell us?'

'I hoped I could avoid the subject, but, some of us, through a cruel caprice of Mother Nature . . .'

'Get to the point.'

'The point is that Tchaikovsky is not an isolated case.'

'You mean – Dr Watson – he is your glass of tea.'

There is no doubt that this scene is funny but the introduction of a homosexual tone in the Holmes and Watson relationship, however comic and light-hearted it may be, does tend to sully it. Quite often there are justifications for altering or enlarging the character of Holmes, but this tampers with legend too much.

Watson is utterly scandalised and outraged when he discovers that Holmes has extricated himself from a delicate situation by pleading homosexuality. He begs for reassurance, asks (in the hope he won't be too presumptuous) if there have not been any women in Holmes's life. Holmes assures Watson that he is being presumptuous.

As if to dispel the suspicion implanted in both our and Watson's mind concerning Holmes's heterosexuality, the story now moves into the main mystery which occupies the rest of the film. This case which Watson considers, 'the most outrageous in all our years together', involves Holmes in becoming romantically attached to a member of the opposite sex.

It all begins when a beautiful young woman (Genevieve Page) arrives on the doorsteps of 221b Baker Street. She apparently has been fished from the Thames suffering from amnesia and with Holmes's address clutched in her hand.

Holmes discovers she has the imprint of a left luggage ticket on the inside of her palm. As he later tells Watson: 'I found her body quite rewarding'. Holmes retrieves her luggage and from it he is able to establish the woman's identity as Gabrielle Valladon, and that she has come from Belgium to find her missing husband, a mining engineer.

Faced with her luggage, Madame Valladon's memory returns and she is able to tell Holmes about the disappearance of her husband. He had invented a new kind of air pump and had been employed by a British company called Jonah Ltd: 'We had been writing to each other regularly then suddenly, five weeks ago, his letters stopped. I kept on writing – no answer. Finally I decided to go to that address. It's just an empty store. Nobody there. I decided to find Jonah Ltd. No such company exists!'

Holmes, intrigued by the problem, asks Madame Valladon to write again to her husband, including only a blank sheet of paper in the envelope. As he

Robert Stephens, Genevieve Page and Colin Blakely in a scene from ***The Private Life of Sherlock Holmes*** **(1970).** *Mirisch*

explains: 'That empty shop is obviously being used as a letter drop. What gets dropped must be picked up. The question is how, and by whom and why?'

The three of them break in at the rear of the empty shop which contains a large cage full of canaries. At the sound of voices they conceal themselves and two men, and an old lady in a wheelchair enter. They transfer a dozen canaries to a smaller cage and leave without touching the letter that lies by the door.

When Watson ponders where the canaries can be bound, Holmes confidently assures him that it will be Inverness: 'Didn't you notice the newspaper in the bottom of the smaller birdcage? It was the "Inverness Courier".'

Meanwhile Madame Valladon has been examining the letter and finds it is addressed to Holmes. He quickly opens it and reads: 'My dear Sherlock, I expect you and Doctor Watson to join me at the club immediately upon receipt of this note. According to my calculations that should be at 11.40 AM. Your brother Mycroft.'

'What time is it, Watson?'

'11.43.'

'Either your watch is wrong or Mycroft miscalculated, and knowing Mycroft, I suggest you reset your watch.'

Holmes and Watson keep their appointment at the Diogenese Club with Mycroft (a slender version played by a bald Christopher Lee). After cordialities, Mycroft warns Holmes not to carry on his search for the mining engineer. Before he can continue a messenger enters with a telegram for him which requires an immediate answer. 'Tell them that the three boxes go to Glennahurrich and the red runner goes to the castle', replies Mycroft and then turns to his brother again. 'When I said you should drop this case it was not merely a suggestion, it was an order.'

'Oh! By whose authority?'

'By the authority of Her Majesty's Government. I hope I make myself clear.'

But of course, it takes more than such a warning to put Holmes off the trail when the game's afoot. That night Holmes and Watson are seen waving goodbye to Madame Valladon at Victoria Station. At eight o'clock Mr and Mrs Ashdown, accompanied by their valet, John, appear at Euston Station and board the Highland Express for Inverness. Watson is the valet, while Holmes plays Mister, to Madame Valladon's Mrs Ashdown. While they share comfortable first class married quarters on the train, Watson, in his role of valet, spends the night on hard seats in the third class, where he ponders whether Holmes is really interested in finding the missing engineer, or is it the engineer's wife that intrigues him so much.

At Glennahurrich the trio witness an unusual funeral. The pall bearers carry three coffins, one of normal size and two smaller ones.

'Holmes!' exclaims Watson. 'Your brother's instructions, remember –

the three boxes to Glennahurrich.'

'I should think you have it,' nods Holmes composedly.

That night Holmes and Watson visit the graveyard and open the coffins. The two smaller ones contain the dead bodies of midgets, while the other contains the body of Emil Valladon, at whose feet are lain six dead canaries, their once bright plumage bleached to a grey white.

Holmes observes that Valladon's copper wedding ring has turned green. 'What does it mean?' asks Watson.

'It means, as I rather expected, that the cause of Emil Valladon's death was most probably not drowning as suggested.'

'What caused this unfortunate lady's husband's death then?'

'Asphyxiation. There is only one substance which can turn copper green and bleach the colour from the feathers of canaries – chlorine gas.'

Holmes then attempts to follow up their only remaining clue: Mycroft's reference to a castle. They visit many in the area, but when Holmes sees Urquhart Castle on the banks of Loch Lomond, he is certain this is the one. They are told the castle is being restored by the Society for the Preservation of Scottish Monuments and entry is barred to them. So at night Holmes, Watson and Madame Valladon spy on the castle from the loch. However, their small boat is overturned by what appears to be the legendary Loch Ness monster.

They manage to reach the shore safely and on returning to the hotel where they are staying, Holmes finds there is a carriage waiting to take him to the castle.

On arriving, he observes a long red carpet being lain by the entrance of a Marquee by the castle wall. On leaving the carriage he is met by his brother, Mycroft, who asks 'Mr Ashdown, I presume?'

'The Red Runner, I presume' declares the detective, indicating the carpet.

Sherlock is shown by his brother into the Marquee.

'How much do you know – or think you know?' asks the irate Mycroft.

'I think you are testing some sort of underwater craft camouflaged to mislead the gullible. I think it is an experimental model operated by a crew of midgets. I think it is powered by sulphuric acid batteries and uses canaries to detect escaping gas. Altogether a unique contraption.'

'Not quite that unique,' corrects Mycroft. 'At this moment four countries are trying to develop what we call, a submersible. So far none of them has been able to solve the critical problem – how to stay submerged long enough for it to be effective.'

'What does the good book say? And Jonah lived in the belly of the fish for three days and three nights.'

'That was our goal, and thanks to Valladon's air pump we got the jump on the rest of them. It is a highly complex system of filtration, so we had a series of trials.'

'And at least one error.'

Mycroft nods seriously and reveals that during a test in the Moray Firth pressure caused a leak in the hull where sea water got in and mixed with the acid in the batteries producing chlorine gas.

'Before they could surface, Valladon and two of the crew were dead.'

'So you had them buried in unmarked graves to preserve your secret,' snaps Sherlock.

'It was essential to keep the information from your client.'

'You went to all those lengths to prevent Madame Valladon from finding her husband?'

'Your client isn't Madame Valladon. It's the Imperial German Government. They were after the Belgian engineer, or rather his invention. They knew he was employed by us, but they could not find out where, so they enlisted you, the best brain in England, to help them. You, my dear brother, have been working for the Wilhelmstrasse.'

Sherlock is visibly shaken, but Mycroft has more to reveal. He informs his brother that the real Madame Valladon is dead, and that the woman who has been impersonating her is Ilse Von Hoffmannsthal, one of Germany's most accomplished spies.

It becomes apparent to the detective that he has been fooled, and fooled by the woman who, it seemed, would replace Irene Adler as 'the woman'. Whatever Sherlock Holmes's feelings are regarding the opposite sex, he certainly had been enjoying his role of Mr Ashdown.

Before he can shake himself from his gloom, Queen Victoria (Mollie Maureen), the real reason for the red runner, arrives to view the submersible. This royal personage, on being informed that the underwater craft is to be used as a warship, carrying torpedoes, is far from amused and orders it to be scrapped.

This prompts Sherlock to point out to his brother, after the Queen has left: 'Well, Mycroft, it seems we've both been undone by a woman'.

The film now rapidly comes to a conclusion. At the request of Sherlock Holmes, the pretty spy is exchanged with the Germans for 'one of our agents' and so at least he saves her the fate of languishing in a damp British prison. At their parting little is said, but their eyes seem to relay unspoken messages to each other.

Months later in Baker Street, Holmes receives a letter from Mycroft:

My Dear Sherlock,

My sources in Tokyo inform me that Ilse Von Hoffmannsthal was arrested last week by the Japanese counter-intelligence service for spying on naval installations in Yokohama harbour. After a secret trial she was summarily executed by firing squad.

It might interest you to know that she had been living in Japan for these past months under the name of Mrs Ashdown.

Yours,
Mycroft.

As Holmes reads the letter an expression of deep sadness fills his face. He stares blankly for a few moments and then, leaving the breakfast table, he heads in the direction of his cocaine supply. And so the film ends.

The suggestion of the romance between the great detective and Madame Valladon, the main aspect surely of the 'Private Life' indicated by the title, is so subtle at times as to be downright vague. Margaret Tarrant wrote in her review of the film in *Films and Filming*: 'Robert Stephens and Genevieve Page fail to convey the growing intensity of the relationship silently developing between them.' As a result, some of Holmes's actions appear obscure and his failure unnecessary.

The film is far too leisurely to excite and Wilder's usually racy wit is not only diluted by the Victorian era, but also by the pacing of the film. And probably it is the time that it takes to get to the point in what is, after all by Holmes's standards, a simple mystery, that made it impossible to include the complete shooting script in the release print. Where, for example, are the scenes of Holmes's University life and how were they to be used in the film? There is a dispute among Sherlockians as to whether Holmes graced Oxford or Cambridge with his presence. Wilder boldly plumps for the former. What happened to the sequence with Lestrade (George Benson) and the case of the upside-down room? We shall, I fear, never know.

Whilst the basic premise is interesting, the film fails to live up to it. Wilder seems vague in which direction the film should go and inevitably it misses all targets. It is too limp for satire, too leisured for a comedy, and far too frivolous to be a thriller. There are, however, some good scenes, in particular the first one discussed earlier, and some of the Holmes and Watson exchanges are amusing.

Holmes: What's that noise?
Watson: Mrs Hudson is entertaining.
Holmes: I have not found her so.

Wilder and Diamond also come up with one or two authentic sounding Holmesisms: 'The art of concealment is being in the right place at the right time.' But they do not seem part of a unified whole.

Strangely enough Wilder is most successful in the middle scenes featuring Holmes's detective work, and this coupled with the way he has managed, however fleetingly, to capture the essence of the period, can only make one regret that he did not try to present a straight Holmes movie.

What of the performances? Christopher Lee appears to play it straight and sans toupee as Mycroft and one reviewer noted that after this performance: 'It should be the end of [his] shoddy Draculas.' Colin Blakely makes a fine comic Watson and in different circumstances, with more restraint, he could present a very authentic version of the doctor.

Robert Stephens, as Holmes, is, on the whole, disappointing. He presents a far too romantic picture of Holmes with his easy movements, nasal drawl and wavy hair. His performance would have suited a portrayal of Oscar Wilde rather than Sherlock Holmes.

However the film did on the whole receive kind and considered reviews. Richard Coombs writing in the *British Monthly Film Bulletin* referred to it as a 'distinctive comedy' while *Films and Filming* placed it in their recommended category.

Despite the encouraging reviews the film met virtually no response from the moviegoers and received sparse bookings. It has now joined the legion of films which are the staple for film societies.

Joanne Woodward (Dr Mildred Watson) and George C. Scott (Justin Playfair) in a scene from *They Might Be Giants* (1972). *Universal*

Chapter 14

'The Old Wheel Turns'

FILM historian William K. Everson notes in his excellent book *The Detective in Film* that:

> . . . since in the seventies the detective film was more and more emphasising speed, action, violence, sex, and the kind of ultra modern and flashy directorial techniques that would inevitably be alien to a faithful and effective filming of Doyle, it is not surprising that Mr Holmes bade the movies farewell.

Although there have been no straight Holmes movies made for the cinema in the seventies the character has not been absent from the screen. *They Might Be Giants,* which was released in 1972, provided one of the most interesting variations on a Sherlockian theme.

The story set in present day New York centres around Justin Playfair (George C. Scott) who, since his wife's death, has withdrawn into a private fantasy in which he dresses, speaks and behaves like Sherlock Holmes. His brother hopes to have Justin committed to an asylum so that he can take over the estate and he is spurred on in this resolution when he comes under a threat of blackmail. Taken to a clinic for analysis, Justin encounters Dr Mildred Watson (Joanne Woodward). He fascinates her by an authoritative Sherlockian diagnosis of one of her patients – a large, lumbering Mr Small who persists in refusing to speak. Justin establishes that Mr Small believes he is Rudolph Valentino and, as a silent star, finds if unnecessary to speak.

Eager to take on this classic case of paranoia, Dr Watson calls on Justin at home where she finds him ensconced in his study which is a replica of Holmes's Baker Street room. She is swiftly disconcerted by Justin's authentic and acute analysis of her own mental state. However, on hearing her name, Justin believes that fate has provided him with his long awaited Watson, and he persuades her to join him in his pursuit of the dreaded Moriarty.

While they wander around New York following the trail that Justin conjures up, a blackmailer tracks them with a view to helping Justin's brother more speedily into his inheritance. Accompanying Justin, Dr Watson discovers that he is completely accepted as Sherlock Holmes by a group of unhappy urbanites who believe in the reality of this noble character. In a sense this provides a partial explanation for the continuing popularity of Holmes and why letters still arrive at his Baker Street address. The qualities embodied in the character of Sherlock Holmes engender a desire in many people to believe in him as a real person, and he remains for them, as he was for Watson, '. . . the best and wisest man whom I have ever known'.

Finally, Justin and Watson follow a clue to Central Park. As they wait there in the darkness for Moriarty, they hear the clip clop and jingle of a hansom cab's horse and a bright light shines ahead of them. It would seem that for them Moriarty does exist and the final impression is of something immense coming to them out of the night.

The film is a delightful piece of whimsy with George C. Scott and Joanne Woodward giving extremely sensitive performances. Scott is too American to be regarded as an authentic Holmes, but of course, this is not the intention of the film. There is one charming sequence where Justin and Watson on the run bump into a police officer who, on observing Justin's Inverness cape and deerstalker, touches his cap and says, 'Oh Mr Rathbone, this is an honour, sir'.

James Goldman's screenplay presents the imaginary Moriarty figure as a symbol of absolute, all-pervading evil, while the Justin Playfair/Sherlock Holmes character represents good fighting alone in an uncomprehending world. Justin also has elements of Don Quixote. Quixote was, of course, crazy to see all windmills as giants; the point Justin asserts is that one of them might be. The film, alas, proved too gentle for modern popular tastes and received only sparse showings.

Also in 1972, Universal, perhaps stuck for something better to do, resurrected *The Hound of the Baskervilles* as one of their movies for television. This production was the pilot for a projected Sherlock Holmes series, but lukewarm reviews and apathetic ratings put an end to that idea.

It was a cheap and shoddy production. One American reviewer wrote that the outdoor moor sets were so bad they seemed to have been borrowed from a children's show: 'the stars were so obviously tramping through plastic.' There were brave attempts to show London street scenes but the lack of authenticity is obvious. Universal utilised some of their mid-European sets used in the horror films of the thirties and forties in which the architecture was far too florid for Victorian London. The Royal Museum of Natural History visited by Holmes in the early stages of the story resembled an Italian railway station.

The script is so convoluted it renders the story incomprehensible. The hound itself is treated in such a desultory fashion that it seems as though its presence was added as an after thought.

Stewart Granger turns in an incredibly flat performance as Holmes. Incongruous with white hair, he presents the detective without any of the individual traits that make Holmes a unique character. Holmes's town clothes are startlingly inaccurate and more reminiscent of a Mississippi gambler than a Victorian consulting detective. Bernard Fox must rate as the most boring Watson ever. Neither completely straight nor a total buffoon, his performance is vague and uninteresting.

The rest of the cast, which included William Shatner as Stapleton, fought vainly against their American accents. It was a thorough disappointment, although *Variety* said in its review of the movie: 'The plot did suggest that there might still be some mileage left in the Holmes mystique with tighter scripting and more attention paid to Holmes's cerebal machinations as an audience challenge.'

In 1975 another attempt was made to get some mileage out of the Holmes mystique, this time for comic purposes, in the film *The Adventure of Sherlock Holmes' Smarter Brother*. The brother in question is not Mycroft, but Sigerson Holmes, the creation of the American comic actor Gene Wilder who wrote and directed the film, as well as playing the leading role.

Unlike *The Private Life of Sherlock Holmes*, this comedy makes no real attempt at pastiche. After the initial spate of Holmes jokes including a reference to 'The Case of the Three Testicles', the film develops into less of a Sherlockian spoof and more into a manic farce with elements of Victorian melodrama.

Gene Wilder seems to have been unable to find the right style for the project and he fails to capture the ethos of the Holmes genre in the way that Mel Brooks so beautifully caught the atmosphere of the old horror movies in *Young Frankenstein*. Wilder also starred in Brooks's film and the tense, exaggerated performance he gave in this is repeated in *The Adventure of Sherlock Holmes' Smarter Brother*.

The story concerns Sigerson's attempts to retrieve the highly important Redcliff documents, the contents of which are never revealed. Also in pursuit of these precious papers is Professor Moriarty. Leo McKern provides a fine, comic, face-twitching Moriarty, a villain who must do 'something absolutely rotten every twenty-four minutes'. Sigerson's investigations involve him with Jenny (Madeline Kahn) who provides the lust interest in the film. She is a music hall singer, governess to the foreign secretary's children and a woman with a past, but not much of a future if Moriarty has anything to do with it.

The irony is, that while Sigerson does all the work and takes all the risks, it is Sherlock, a shadowy background figure throughout, who steps in at the end to collect the papers and the praise. Sigerson, however, gets the girl.

Sigerson's assistant, played by Marty Feldman, is called Ormond Sacker which is a sort of in-joke for Sherlockians, this being Conan Doyle's original name for Dr Watson.

The real Holmes and Watson do appear briefly at the opening of the film.

Sigi Holmes (Gene Wilder) and Moriarty's henchman (Roy Kinnear) fight it out atop a hansom cab in *The Adventure of Sherlock Holmes' Smarter Brother* **(1975).** *Fox Rank*

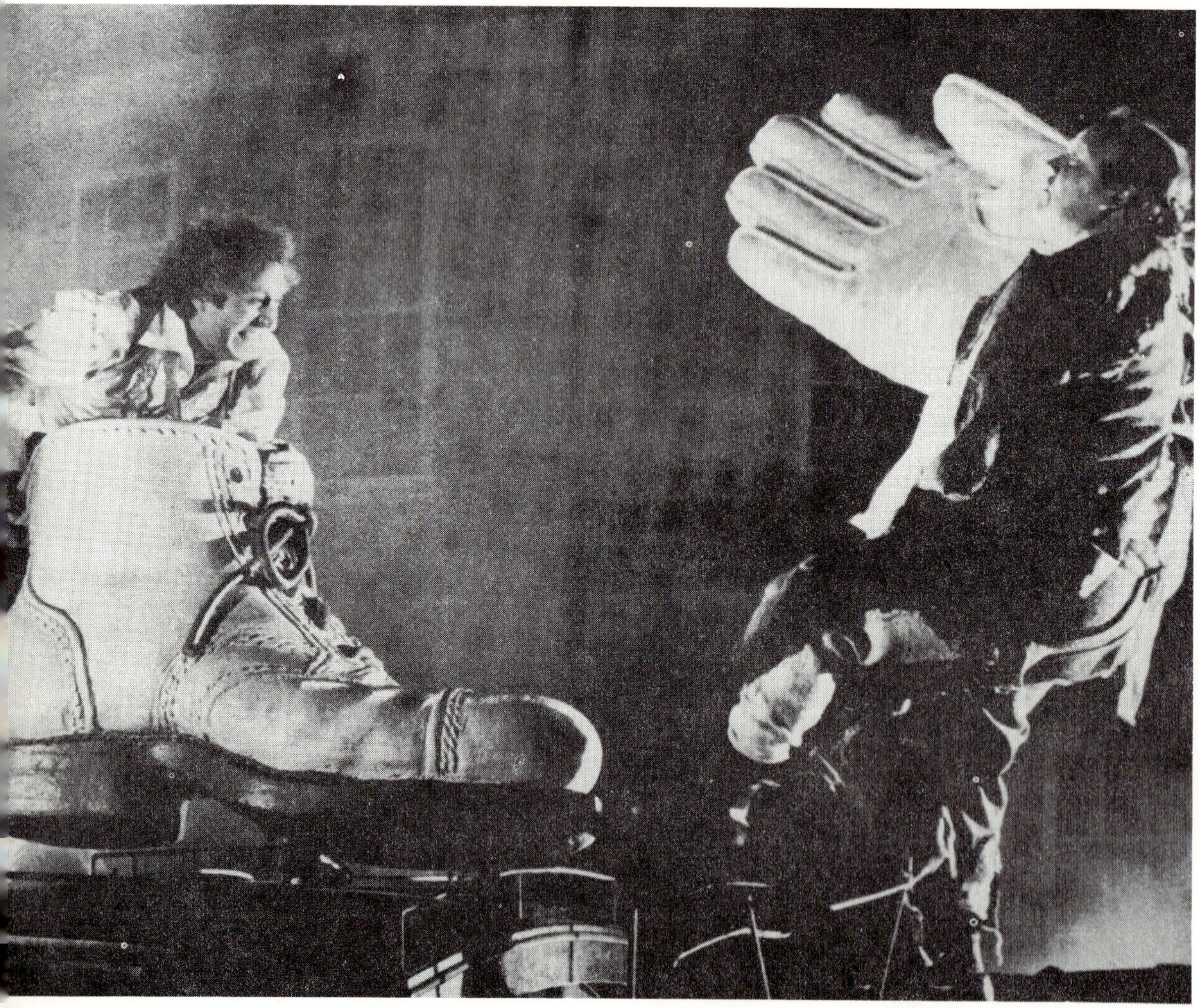

The detective is played almost straight by Douglas Wilmer who is no stranger to the part having been a very effective Holmes in the first BBC television series in 1965, while Thorley Walters' portrayal of Watson is almost identical to the one he gave in *Sherlock Holmes and the Deadly Necklace.*

Late 1976 promises yet another Holmes comedy with a film based on Nicholas Meyer's book, *The Seven Per Cent Solution.* In the novel, Meyer fills in the missing months in Holmes's career after he plunged over the Reichenbach falls wrestling with Moriarty and before he made his reappearance ready to start work again. The plot not only involves the detective doing battle with Moriarty,

Sigi (Gene Wilder) and Orville Sacker (Marty Feldman) discovered eavesdropping by Moriarty (Leo McKern) and accomplice in *The Adventure of Sherlock Holmes' Smarter Brother* **(1975).** *Fox Rank*

but also has him attending Sigmund Freud's clinic in Vienna. The whole story purports to come from a memoir written by Watson but not disclosed until long after the detective's demise and when Watson himself is on the verge of death.

Despite the liberties taken with the legend in the book it is written more or less straight in the Conan Doyle style, but the film publicists are talking about the movie version in terms of a stylised and 'hard-edged comedy'. The part of Holmes is in the hands of Nicol Williamson whose approach to the character is rather surprising. He has admitted to having never seen a Holmes movie nor read any of Conan Doyle's tales. This start-from-scratch approach tends to diminish the original conception of the character. Sherlock Holmes is only Sherlock Holmes because he possesses the unique characteristics given him by Conan Doyle. If no attempt is made to reproduce these on screen there seems little point in calling the character Sherlock Holmes.

However, the film's director Herbert Ross has an affection for the detective and believes that Holmes 'embodies all the perfect ideals of mankind dedicated to the punishment of injustice'. With the film in the hands of a man who holds this view perhaps the completed movie may not be as un-Sherlockian as first imagined.

The Seven Per Cent Solution boasts a starry cast which includes Vanessa Redgrave, Jeremy Kemp, Samantha Eggar, and Robert Duvall as Watson and Sir Laurence Olivier as Professor Moriarty.

Where does Holmes of the movies go from here? Despite the fact that he has been featured in two major productions within a year, indicating a revival of interest in the character, there appears little likelihood of a straight Holmes feature being made at the present time. For this we must look to the future, for as long as there is a penchant for Sherlockian spoofs, the serious Holmes movie will remain a box office risk which film companies will not be prepared to take.

However, public taste is fickle, and as the Master himself notes in *The Valley of Fear*: 'Everything comes in circles. The old wheel turns and the same spoke comes up'. As contemporary life becomes more and more uncertain and unsettled we will feel a greater urge to indulge ourselves in nostalgia for past golden ages when the world seemed more relaxed and leisurely. Sherlock Holmes remains a fixed point in our changing age so, who knows, we may at any time see a genuine Holmes revival.

I would rather believe that, far from retiring from the screen, Mr Holmes is just waiting off set for his cue to re-enter. While both he and we wait for this to happen we can keep our eye on the television papers in the hope of catching one of the old features, so that we can once again enjoy the thrills and the magic of Holmes of the movies.

Filmography

A checklist of the major movies covered in the text.
** denotes titles issued in Great Britain*

THE SILENT FEATURES

1903 *Sherlock Holmes Baffled* (USA) The American Mutoscope and Bioscope Co.

1905 *The Adventures of Sherlock Holmes* or *Held for a Ransom* (USA) *Sherlock Holmes* or *Held for Ransom* (GB) The Vitagraph Co.
Director: J. Stuart Blackton
Screenplay: Theodor Liebler
Sherlock Holmes: Maurice Costello

1908 *Sherlock Holmes and the Great Murder Mystery* (USA) Crescent Film Co.

1908 *Rival Sherlock Holmes* (Italy) Ambrosio.

The Nordisk Film Company series (Denmark)

Titles include:
1908 **Sherlock Holmes*
1908 **Sherlock Holmes in the Gas Cellar*
Sherlock Holmes: Viggo Larsen
1909 **The Theft of the Diamonds*
1910 **The Murder in Baker Street*
1911 **The Hotel Mystery* or *Sherlock Holmes's Last Exploits* or *Hotel Rats*
Director: Forrect Holger-Madsen
Sherlock Holmes: Forrect Holger-Madsen or Viggo Larsen (see above)
Dr Watson: Alwin Neuss

The Eclair Anglo-French series of two-reelers (with the cooperation of Conan Doyle)

Titles include:
1912 **The Speckled Band*
1912 **The Beryl Coronet*
1912 **Silver Blaze*
1913 **The Reigate Squires*
1913 **The Adventure of the Copper Beeches*
1913 **The Mystery of Boscombe Vale*
1913 **The Stolen Papers*
1913 **The Musgrave Ritual*
Director: Georges Treville (with the cooperation of Conan Doyle)
Sherlock Holmes: Georges Treville

1914 *A Study in Scarlet* (GB) The Samuelson Film Mfg Co Ltd.
Director: George Pearson
Screenplay: Harry Engholm
Sherlock Holmes: James Bragington

1916 *The Valley of Fear* (GB) The Samuelson Film Mfg Co Ltd.
Director: Alexander Butler
Screenplay: Harry Engholm
Sherlock Holmes: H. A. Saintsbury
Dr Watson: Arthur M. Cullin
Prof Moriarty: Booth Conway

1916 *Sherlock Holmes* (USA) Essanay.
Director: Arthur Berthelet
Screenplay: H. S. Sheldon (from Conan Doyle and Gillette's stage play)
Sherlock Holmes: William Gillette
Dr Watson: Edward Fielding
Prof Moriarty: Ernest Maupin

Stoll Picture Productions Ltd, first series

1921 *Adventures of Sherlock Holmes* (GB) (series title)
The Dying Detective
The Devil's Foot
A Case of Identity
The Yellow Face
The Red-Headed League
The Resident Patient
A Scandal in Bohemia

The Man with the Twisted Lip
The Beryl Coronet
The Noble Bachelor
The Copper Beeches
The Empty House
The Tiger of San Pedro (based on *Wisteria Lodge*)
The Priory School
The Solitary Cyclist
Director: Maurice Elvey
Screenplays: William J. Elliot and Maurice Elvey
Sherlock Holmes: Eille Norwood
Dr Watson: Hubert Willis

1921 *The Hound of the Baskervilles* (GB) Stoll Picture Productions Ltd.
Director: Maurice Elvey
Screenplay: William J. Elliot
Sherlock Holmes: Eille Norwood
Dr Watson: Hubert Willis
Dr Mortimer: Alan Jeayes
Sir Henry Baskerville: Rex McDougall
Stapleton: Lewis Gilbert
Mrs Hudson: Madame d'Esterre

Stoll Picture Productions Ltd, second series

1922 *Further Adventures of Sherlock Holmes* (GB) (series title)
Charles Augustus Milverton
The Abbey Grange
The Norwood Builder
The Reigate Squires
The Naval Treaty
The Second Stain
The Red Circle
The Six Napoleons
Black Peter
The Bruce-Partington Plans
The Stockbroker's Clerk
The Boscombe Valley Mystery
The Musgrave Ritual
The Golden Pince-nez
The Greek Interpreter
Director: George Ridgewell
Screenplays: Patrick L. Mannock and Geoffrey H. Malins
Sherlock Holmes: Eille Norwood

Dr Watson: Hubert Willis

1922 *Sherlock Holmes* (USA) *Moriarty* (GB) Goldwyn Pictures.
Director: Albert Parker
Sherlock Holmes: John Barrymore
Dr Watson: Ronald Young
Prof Moriarty: Gustav von Seyffertitz
Alice Faulkener: Carol Dempster

Stoll Picture Productions Ltd, third series

1923 *The Last Adventures of Sherlock Holmes* (GB) (series title)
Silver Blaze
The Speckled Band
The Gloria Scott
The Blue Carbuncle
The Engineer's Thumb
His Last Bow
The Cardboard Box
The Disappearance of Lady Frances Carfax
The Three Students
The Missing Three-Quarter
The Mystery of Thor Bridge
The Stone of Mazarin
The Dancing Men
The Crooked Man
The Final Problem
Director: George Ridgewell
Screenplays: Geoffrey H. Malins and P. L. Mannock
Sherlock Holmes: Eille Norwood
Dr Watson: Hubert Willis
Prof Moriarty: Percy Standing

1923 *The Sign of Four* (GB) Stoll Picture Productions Ltd.
Director: Maurice Elvey
Screenplay: Maurice Elvey
Sherlock Holmes: Eille Norwood
Dr Watson: Arthur Cullin (replacing Hubert Willis who was thought to be too old for the romantic element)
Mary Morstan: Isobel Elsom
Mrs Hudson: Madame d'Esterre

THE SOUND FEATURES

1929 *The Return of Sherlock Holmes* (USA) Paramount.
Director: Basil Dean (with Clive Brook)
Screenplay: Basil Dean and Garret Fort
Sherlock Holmes: Clive Brook
Dr Watson: H. Reeves Smith
Prof Moriarty: Harry T. Morey
Col Sebastian Moran: Donald Crisp
Mary Watson: Betty Lawford

1931 *The Sleeping Cardinal* (GB) *Sherlock Holmes's Fatal Hour* (USA) Twickenham Film Studios Ltd.
Director: Leslie Hiscott
Screenplay: Leslie Hiscott and Cyril Twyford
Sherlock Holmes: Arthur Wontner
Dr Watson: Ian Fleming
Mrs Hudson: Minnie Rayner
Col Sebastian Moran: Louis Goodrich
Insp Lestrade: Philip Hewland

1931 *The Speckled Band* (GB) British and Dominion.
Director: Jack Raymond
Screenplay: W. P. Liscomb
Sherlock Holmes: Raymond Massey
Dr Watson: Athole Stewart
Dr Rylott: Lyn Harding

1932 *The Hound of the Baskervilles* (GB) Gainsborough Pictures.
Director: Gareth Gundrey
Screenplay: Edgar Wallace and Gareth Gundrey
Sherlock Holmes: Robert Rendel
Dr Watson: Fred Lloyd
Sir Henry Baskerville: John Stuart
Stapleton: Reginald Bach
Dr Mortimer: Wilfred Shine
Sir Hugo Baskerville: Sam Livesy
Barrymore: Henry Hallatt

1932 *The Missing Rembrandt* (GB) Twickenham Film Studios Ltd.
Director: Leslie Hiscott
Screenplay: H. Fowler Mear and Cyril Twyford (loosely based on *Charles Augustus Milverton*)

Sherlock Holmes: Arthur Wontner
Dr Watson: Ian Fleming
Mrs Hudson: Minnie Rayner
Insp Lestrade: Philip Hewland

1932 *The Sign of Four* (GB) Associated Radio Pictures.
Director: Graham Cutts
Screenplay: W. P. Liscomb
Sherlock Holmes: Arthur Wontner
Dr Watson: Ian Hunter
Mrs Hudson: Claire Greet

1932 *Sherlock Holmes* (USA) Fox.
Director: William K. Howard
Screenplay: Bertram Millhauser
Sherlock Holmes: Clive Brook
Dr Watson: Reginald Owen
Alice Faulkener: Miriam Jordan
Prof Moriarty: Ernest Torrence

1933 *A Study in Scarlet* (USA) Worldwide.
Director: Edwin L. Marin
Screenplay: Robert Florey, with additional dialogue by Reginald Owen
Sherlock Holmes: Reginald Owen
Dr Watson: Warburton Gamble
Mrs Hudson: Tempe Pigott
Insp Lestrade: Alan Mowbray

1935 *The Triumph of Sherlock Holmes* (GB) Real Art Productions Ltd.
Director: Leslie Hiscott
Screenplay: H. Fowler Mear and Cyril Twyford (loosely based on *The Valley of Fear*).
Sherlock Holmes: Arthur Wontner
Dr Watson: Ian Fleming
Mrs Hudson: Minnie Rayner
Insp Lestrade: Charles Mortimer
Prof Moriarty: Lyn Harding
Col Sebastian Moran: Arthur Coullett

1937 *Silver Blaze* (GB) *Murder at the Baskervilles* (USA)
Twickenham Film Productions Ltd.
Director: Thomas Bentley

Screenplay: H. Fowler Mear and Arthur Macrae
Sherlock Holmes: Arthur Wontner
Dr Watson: Ian Fleming
Prof Moriarty: Lyn Harding
Insp Lestrade: John Turnbull
Col Sebastian Moran: Arthur Coullett

1939 *The Hound of the Baskervilles* (USA) Twentieth Century Fox.
Director: Sidney Lanfield
Screenplay: Ernest Pascal
Sherlock Holmes: Basil Rathbone
Dr Watson: Nigel Bruce
Sir Henry Baskerville: Richard Greene
Beryl Stapleton: Wendy Barrie
Dr Mortimer: Lionel Atwill
Barryman: John Carradine
Mrs Hudson: Mary Gordon
John Stapleton: Martin Lowry

1939 *The Adventures of Sherlock Holmes* (USA) Twentieth Century Fox.
Director: Alfred Werker
Screenplay: Edwin Blum and William Drake
Sherlock Holmes: Basil Rathbone
Dr Watson: Nigel Bruce
Ann Brandon: Ida Lupino
Prof Moriarty: George Zucco
Insp Bristol: E. E. Clive
Mrs Hudson: Mary Gordon

The Universal Series (USA)

1942 *Sherlock Holmes and the Voice of Terror*
Director: John Rawlins
Screenplay: Lynn Riggs and Robert D. Andrews
Sherlock Holmes: Basil Rathbone
Dr Watson: Nigel Bruce
Kitty: Evelyn Ankers
Sir Evan Barham: Reginald Denny
Anthony Lloyd: Henry Daniell
Mrs Hudson: Mary Gordon

1942 *Sherlock Holmes and the Secret Weapon* (working title: *Sherlock Holmes Fights Back*)
Director: Roy William Neill

Screenplay: Edward T. Lloyd, W. Scott Darling and Edmund L. Hartmann
Sherlock Holmes: Basil Rathbone
Dr Watson: Nigel Bruce
Prof Moriarty: Lionel Atwill
Dr Franz Tobel: William Post Jnr

1943 *Sherlock Holmes in Washington*
Director: Roy William Neill
Screenplay: Bertram Millhauser and Lynn Riggs (from a story by Bertram Millhauser)
Sherlock Holmes: Basil Rathbone
Dr Watson: Nigel Bruce
William Raster: Henry Daniell
Stanley: George Zucco
Nancy Partridge: Majorie Lord
Senator Babock: Thurston Hall

1943 *Sherlock Holmes Faces Death*
Director/Producer: Roy William Neill
Screenplay: Bertram Millhauser (loosely based on *The Musgrave Ritual*)
Sherlock Holmes: Basil Rathbone
Dr Watson: Nigel Bruce
Sally Musgrave: Hillary Brooke
Dr Sexton: Arthur Margetson
Captain Vickery: Milburn Stone
Insp Lestrade: Dennis Hoey
Mrs Hudson: Mary Gordon

1944 *Spider Woman*
Director/Producer: Roy William Neill
Screenplay: Bertram Millhauser
Sherlock Holmes: Basil Rathbone
Dr Watson: Nigel Bruce
Andrea Spedding: Gale Sondergaard
Norman: Vernon Downing
Insp Lestrade: Dennis Hoey
Mrs Hudson: Mary Gordon

1944 *The Scarlet Claw*
Director/Producer: Roy William Neill
Screenplay: Edmund L. Hartmann and Roy William Neill

(from a story by Paul Gangelin and Brenda Weisberg)
Sherlock Holmes: Basil Rathbone
Dr Watson: Nigel Bruce
Alistair Ramson/Potts/Tanner: Gerald Hamer
Lord Penrose: Paul Cavanagh
Journet: Arthur Hohl
Judge Brisson: Miles Mander
Marie: Kay Harding
Sgt Thompson: David Clyde

1944 *The Pearl of Death*
Director/Producer: William Roy Neill
Screenplay: Bertram Millhauser (loosely based on *The Six Napoleons*)
Sherlock Holmes: Basil Rathbone
Dr Watson: Nigel Bruce
Giles Conover: Miles Mander
Naomi Drake: Evelyn Ankers
The Creeper: Rondo Hatton
Insp Lestrade: Dennis Hoey

1945 *The House of Fear*
Director/Producer: Roy William Neill
Screenplay: Roy Chanslor (loosely based on *The Five Orange Pips*)
Sherlock Holmes: Basil Rathbone
Dr Watson: Nigel Stock
Alistair: Aubrey Mather
Dr Merrivale: Paul Cavanagh
Cosgrave: Holmes Herbert
Mrs Monteith: Sally Shepherd
Simpson: Harry Cording
Insp Lestrade: Dennis Hoey

1945 *The Woman in Green*
Director/Producer: Roy William Neill
Screenplay: Bertram Millhauser (loosely based on *The Adventure of the Empty House*)
Sherlock Holmes: Basil Rathbone
Dr Watson: Nigel Bruce
Prof Moriarty: Henry Daniell
Insp Gregson: Matthew Boulton
Lydia: Hillary Brooke
Fenwick: Paul Cavanagh

Maude: Eve Amber
Mrs Hudson: Mary Gordon

1945 *Pursuit to Algiers*
Director/Producer: Roy William Neill
Screenplay: Leonard Lee
Sherlock Holmes: Basil Rathbone
Dr Watson: Nigel Bruce
Sheila: Marjorie Riordan
Mirko: Martin Kosleck
Nikolas: Leslie Vincent
Sanford: Martin Lowry

1946 *Terror by Night*
Director/Producer: Roy William Neill
Screenplay: Frank Gruber
Sherlock Holmes: Basil Rathbone
Dr Watson: Nigel Bruce
Major Duncan Bleek: Alan Mowbray
Vivian Vedder: Renee Godfrey
Lady Margaret: Mary Forbes
Train attendant: Billy Bevan
Sands: Skelton Knaggs
Insp Lestrade: Dennis Hoey

1946 *Dressed to Kill* or *Sherlock Holmes and the Secret Code* (GB)
Director/Producer: Roy William Neill
Screenplay: Leonard Lee
Sherlock Holmes: Basil Rathbone
Dr Watson: Nigel Bruce
Hilda Courtney: Patricia Morison
Julian Emery: Edmund Breon
Col Cavanagh: Frederic Worlock
Insp Hopkins: Carl Harbord
Mrs Hudson: Mary Gordon

1951 *The Man with the Twisted Lip* (GB) Vandyke Pictures.
Director: Richard M. Grey
Sherlock Holmes: John Longdon
Dr Watson: Campbell Singer

1959 *The Hound of the Baskervilles* (GB) Hammer Film Productions Ltd.
(The first Holmes movie to be shot in colour)
Director: Terence Fisher
Screenplay: Peter Bryan
Sherlock Holmes: Peter Cushing
Dr Watson: André Morell
Sir Henry Baskerville: Christopher Lee
Dr Mortimer: Francis de Wolff
Cecile: Marla Landi
Bishop Frankland: Miles Malleson
Stapleton: Ewen Solon
Barrymore: John Le Mesurier
Mrs Barrymore: Helen Goss
Sir Hugo Baskerville: David Oxley

1962 *Sherlock Holmes und das Halsband des Todes* (West Germany)
Sherlock Holmes and the Deadly Necklace (GB 1968) CCC Films.
Director: Terence Fisher
Screenplay: Curt Siodmak
Sherlock Holmes: Christopher Lee
Dr Watson: Thorley Walters
Prof Moriarty: Hans Söhnker
Ellen Blackburn: Senta Berger

1965 *A Study in Terror* (GB) Compton-Cameo Films.
Director: James Hill
Screenplay: Donald Ford and Derek Ford
Sherlock Holmes: John Neville
Dr Watson: Donald Houston
Lord Carfax: John Fraser
Dr Murray: Anthony Quale
Mycroft Holmes: Robert Morley
Angela: Adrienne Corri
Max Steiner: Peter Carsten
Mrs Hudson: Barbara Leake
Insp Lestrade: Frank Finlay

1970 *The Private Life of Sherlock Holmes* (GB) Mirisch Production Co/
United Artists.
Director/Producer: Billy Wilder
Screenplay: Billy Wilder and I. A. L. Diamond
Sherlock Holmes: Robert Stephens
Dr Watson: Colin Blakely

Mrs Hudson: Irene Handl
1st Gravedigger: Stanley Holloway
Mycroft Holmes: Christopher Lee
Gabrielle Valladon: Genevieve Page
Queen Victoria: Mollie Maureen

1972 *They Might Be Giants* (USA) Universal.
Director: Anthony Harvey
Screenplay: James Goldman (based on his own play)
Justin Playfair (Sherlock Holmes): George C. Scott
Dr Mildred Watson: Joanne Woodward

1972 *The Hound of the Baskervilles* (USA) Universal (made for television).
Sherlock Holmes: Stewart Granger
Dr Watson: Bernard Fox
Stapleton: William Shatner
Dr Mortimer: Anthony Zerbe
Laura Frankland: Sally Ann Howes
Sir Henry Baskerville: Ian Ireland

1975 *The Adventure of Sherlock Holmes' Smarter Brother* (USA) A Roth/Jouer Production.
Director: Gene Wilder
Screenplay: Gene Wilder
Producer: Richard A. Roth
Sigerson Holmes: Gene Wilder
Ormond Sacker: Marty Feldman
Jenny: Madeline Kahn
Sherlock Holmes: Douglas Wilmer
Dr Watson: Thorley Walters
Moriarty: Leo McKern

1976 *The Seven Per Cent Solution* Cinema International.
Director: Herbert Ross
Screenplay: from the book by Nicholas Meyer
Sherlock Holmes: Nichol Williamson
Dr Watson: Robert Duvall
Prof Moriarty: Laurence Olivier